Home on the Big

Home on the Big Salmon

Sid Bell

Copyright © 2011 by Sid Bell.

Library of Congress Control Number:		2011906467
ISBN:	Hardcover	978-1-4628-6203-0
	Softcover	978-1-4628-6202-3
	Ebook	978-1-4628-6204-7

This is a work of fiction. Names, characters, places and incidents either are the product of the author's imagination or are used fictitiously, and any resemblance to any actual persons, living or dead, events, or locales is entirely coincidental.

This book was printed in the United States of America.

To order additional copies of this book, contact:
Xlibris Corporation
1-888-795-4274
www.Xlibris.com
Orders@Xlibris.com
96277

PART 1

CHAPTER 1

THE RAIN CONTINUED to fall as it had done for three long days. Bob Walker walked slowly down the ramp, savoring every moment of this, his homecoming. Even though the conditions were not what he had hoped for, his spirit could not be dampened. A smile was on his lips, a song in his heart, and determination on his mind.

It was October 1945. The war was over, and the boys were coming home. Bob was one of those boys, only he wasn't a boy anymore. Nearly four years ago he had volunteered his services to a cause he'd thought to be worthy. Being just a boy with stars in his eyes, he had no way of knowing what lay in store for himself and the others. On a spring day in 1942, the war had begun for Bob. It was some months earlier that he had enlisted, but he was still a runny-nosed kid when the troop carrier hit the shore. Like players in a game of tag, the young soldiers started running up the beach. This was not much different than basic training had been, Bob thought, as he continued toward the trees and the cover they'd provide.

Then he heard the engines and recognized the sound of German planes. Bob fell to the ground and lay there as the fighters cut the ground forces to ribbons. When the smoke cleared, the few who remained could not believe it. In just a matter of a few moments, they were all but wiped out. Many of the young men were dead; more were badly wounded. Those who were unhurt could not fathom what had just taken place. Bob was among those who had gone unscathed, one of the lucky ones, or was he?

A few days after the bombing of Pearl Harbor, he had signed up. From that day in December, he was either being prepared for war or was embroiled in it. Never again could he ever be the happy-go-lucky, carefree individual that he once was. His youth was gone now, lost somewhere along the way—the way being the constant struggle to stay alive in the horror that had been war.

Many things ran through Bob's mind as he stood quietly enjoying the moment. As he looked up and down, the water from his hat, soaked by the rain, began to drip onto his nose, and still he stood there. It was no big thing to be soaked to the skin anymore. Many times he'd lain in a foxhole filled with muddy water. Homesick and frightened, he'd lain there as if alone, though there were always others with him. This was a piece of cake; the rain was warm, and the people were friendly. They were pushing and shoving as they attempted to pass, but there were no grenades or rifles here. He was home, and in spite of the rain, no money, and no job, Bob was glad to be here. War-torn Europe was yesterday; the war was over, and opportunity lay ahead. It was evening, and tomorrow would be another day, one he could look forward to. On the horizon, the sky was beginning to clear; he heard his father yell, "Robert, is that you?" Bob looked up and said, "Thank you, Lord, for everything," then tears began to fall.

The following morning, the sun rose in a clear sky. Bob was still sleeping when his mother answered the knock at the front door. Helen had come for coffee. She was a young girl next door who had become friends with Bob's parents since moving in just two years prior. Bob's mother stood at the bottom of the stairs and called out, "Robert, come have coffee with us, and we have company."

Bob slowly opened his still-heavy eyelids and swung a leg over the side of the bed. As he sat there, a sparrow landed on the windowsill and chirped a song. Not knowing and maybe not caring that Bob was watching, the bird continued to share his happiness with the world. It had been a long time since Bob could remember seeing such a display. It was nice to be home where there was a measure of peace and quiet. Just the fact that this little creature would sit not twenty feet from him and sing out without fear was enough to touch him. This was truly a unique and precious part of the world.

After pulling on his pants, Bob combed his hair and brushed his teeth. The bird's song was still on his mind as he put on his socks and shoes. He pulled on his shirt and ran down the stairs to greet the day. The hint of his once-joyful and carefree manner was beginning, once again, to make itself known. It had lain dormant for some time, and it felt good to anticipate once again the good things life had to offer.

Bob was still on a trot when he got to the bottom of the stairs, whistling a tune as he rounded the corner into the kitchen. "What were you saying, Mom? I couldn't hear you up there."

"We have company, Robert, Helen from next door." Turning to Helen, she said, "This is our son, Robert. He's been away fighting the war, but now he's come back to us."

Helen was a small girl, pretty and quiet. She had black eyes, long eyelashes, a small nose, a noble chin, and a high forehead, which showed her to be a thinker, Bob thought. She had a grin that told him that she knew much more than she was willing to admit. Over coffee, the two young people began to talk of things that were of mutual interest. The weeks went by, and Bob began to appreciate the superior personality of this young lady. He was impressed by that personality, her strong character, sense of purpose, and determination.

CHAPTER 2

YOUNG BOB HAD studied to be a builder before the war began. He went back to school and began to pick up where he had left off. Many new things had to be learned despite the fact that only four years had elapsed since he had first attended trade school. Under wartime conditions, much research had been done, and many new methods were now being used.

The war had left Bob with scars and memories that would not go away quickly. He had to develop techniques of his own to deal with life under peacetime conditions. He had developed into a good soldier—he had to—and he fully intended to come back. He'd learned to go by gut feeling and did not shy away from a good scrap, not then and not now. He had problems dealing with some of his fellow students who did not understand. Bob had been programmed for months to become a fighting machine. It took time to learn to handle that machine in peacetime. Only once did he have to resort to violence, however.

It happened on a day that began badly for Bob. He was late for school and in a poor mood to begin with. Three hardheads confronted him and wouldn't let up. He kept insisting that they go about their own business and stop bothering him. They didn't, and eventually the talking was over. Within minutes, all three were on the floor, holding their stomachs, broken, and bleeding. They didn't bother Bob again, but he had been frightened by it. There was no real lasting damage done, but Bob had lost his temper; somebody could have been killed. It was a lesson he never forgot.

There is a German proverb that states that patience is a bitter plant but it produces a sweet fruit. The proverb proved to be true in Bob's case. His patience and hard work paid off when he received a diploma, and soon he found employment as well. He devised a plan that made it necessary to work for a construction company. He needed practical experience before he could start a business of his own, and working for wages provided the vehicle to carry him toward that objective. Bob threw himself into his work, and it was not long until he had built a good reputation. He became known as one of the best construction men available. The time, however, was not yet right to start a business. The banks were reluctant to lend the kind of money he'd need to an untried contractor. He could start small and spend years building a company, but that was not what he wanted. He also had Helen on his mind more and more lately. The decision was made to continue as he was for a while; after all, he was making a good wage.

Bob was content with his decision to work for wages for a time. He began thinking a good deal about another concern that kept nagging him. His life was beginning to become complicated, and he was not altogether against the idea. The complication came in a package with a brown top and black eyes: Helen. Bob's interest had grown; he was becoming closer to the girl, and she seemed very much in favor. As weeks turned into months, a new chapter was being written in each of their lives.

Helen was a delightful young lady, born and raised in Vancouver. She received her teaching degree at the University of British Columbia and planned to work in Prince George, the home of her parents. Helen had visited there many times, enjoyed the city, and looked forward to residing there once her schooling was complete.

Life, however, is full of surprises. Her father became ill and needed a change of climate, so he moved south to Vancouver. Helen, an only child, came with him and began teaching at an elementary school just a few blocks from their home. As fate would have it, their home just happened to be next door to Bob's parents' house.

Helen grew up loving the wilderness. When her father was healthy, he'd take his family into the wild for days at a time. Even on winter weekends, they'd spent their time cooking on a campfire and sleeping in a tent. As a child, Helen had loved it, and even now, because it could not be, she missed it. She missed the sharing of work that is so vital in that type of situation. Her mother had loved it too; she was gone now, and Helen missed her too. She missed the father that she used to know. The man that her father's health had forced him to become was a shell of what he once was. Often she would sit and think about how unfair life could be. I suppose, the pent-up anger and frustration of it all demanded a release. She found that release lately by drifting away into another world for a time, going back to yesteryear. She saw the two of them driving along a seldom-used road somewhere in the Yukon. How Pop loved the Yukon! He'd planned to live there someday, but talk was all that came of it. Coming to a bridge, he stopped the car, got out, and looked at the gravel on the bottom of the creek. "This is where we stop," he said, and began to take the fishing gear out of the trunk. He then backed the car off to the side of the road, and we began to walk.

"Why did you check the creek bottom, Pop?" Helen asked. She couldn't understand why it would make a difference.

"Ah, there is the secret," he said. "To be a fisherman, one must know something of their habitat. To be a successful fisherman, one must know their habits.

"Today we will fish for arctic grayling. These fish prefer rapids where the water is moving quickly over a gravel bottom. Chances are, there will be grayling near."

They walked down a path that led them into the trees and away from the creek as far as Helen could see. She did not realize then that she and her father were walking along the top of a ridge. The going up here was much easier than trying to follow the creek, which wound down below through thick brush and deadfalls. Soon the path came back to the creek, and because the brush became too thick with its snarls and thickets, they took to the creek bed. Continuing to walk down the creek bed, they shortly came to its mouth and arrived at the location where Gravel Creek joined the Rose River.

Helen chuckled when she remembered the little girl who sat on the shore. Her father had sat her down on the upstream side of the river. She sat quietly as she held on to her fishing rod. Her dad fastened a float to her line about fifteen feet up from the hook, and now she watched intently as the float began to bob up and down. The line went quickly toward the far side of the river, then it stopped, came back, and started up the creek. Helen had been dumbfounded as all she could do was watch. The trance was broken when Dad said, "Reel him in, girl. We won't catch our limit unless we take them off the hook." How she loved those memories of her childhood. Her father was out in the middle of Gravel Creek, standing in a pair of chest waders and snapping out a fly line, when the phone rang and brought her back to reality. The events of the last few years had set the lives of Helen and her father on a different course. Neither would forget the good times spent together, however; they would go on remembering the days of tramping the bush trails and drinking coffee that they'd brewed on the campfire.

She picked up the receiver. "Hello," she said. It was Bob.

"I'll be spending a few days with Mom and Dad. I'm wondering if I can see you."

"Certainly. Come over anytime," she said. They continued to talk. It was during these few days that they each made a decision about one another. Circumstances had undoubtedly led them thus far, but now circumstance would take a backseat. They'd wanted to be together as friends; now friendship had produced a deeper feeling, and each of them knew that only in marriage could they fulfill the feelings that had grown within them.

CHAPTER 3

SOMEONE SAID THAT a man's dying is more the survivor's affair than his own. Such was the case when Helen's father passed on. She had known that he was fading badly; he had been ill for some time, and yet death still came as a shock. The night before, Helen had sat with her father and listened as he slowly spoke of former times. He was not bitter, but neither did he seem to have any hope. He had no assurance that there was life after death, and that was sad. Tears came into Helen's eyes when she left her father's side and entered her bedroom. The next morning, she rose early and went immediately to his room. He had passed away during the night. He had been a good father, a friend. She would miss him.

Bob helped with the funeral arrangements where he could. The proceedings were understandably hard for Helen, and she was most thankful. After the service, they gathered in the home of Bob's parents. Helen made the comment that she was now in the presence of the only family she had left. Bob's mother said, "I'd like that." His father agreed, and so did Bob. Shortly afterward, they were married. In a quiet and tiny ceremony, the two became one flesh, signifying to the world before God and man that they would walk as one from that day forward. They did not go on a honeymoon immediately; they waited for summer, and when it came, they headed north. For years Bob had yearned to visit the Yukon Territory, and Helen was eager to show him areas where she had been as a child. Together they spent two months canoeing and enjoying the majestic beauty of the land of the midnight sun.

On the third day of July, the sun was high in a clear blue sky when they reached Vancouver. Helen contacted a girlfriend from school and spent the afternoon with her. They stayed in the city that night and left the following morning.

It was evening on the third day after leaving Vancouver that they arrived in Watson Lake. They had arrived! Bob was in the part of the world he had long dreamed of. They both had contemplated this moment for some time. Before falling asleep, exhausted, they retraced the route that they had planned to follow.

Morning came, and they headed west on the Alaska Highway, stopping at each creek and river along the way. They could not continue their way, feeling that there might have been a fish they could have caught. Many fish were caught and of course released; they kept only those they could eat along the way. It became harder to leave each campsite when morning would arrive. The two youngsters were thoroughly enjoying themselves, and the days slipped away very quickly.

Almost a week had passed when they arrived in Teslin, a small community nestled in the trees on the shores of Teslin Lake. They stopped and talked to some local residents about the main focus of their vacation.

Just a few miles west, the highway crossed over the Teslin River. The South Canol Road began its winding way north from the east side of the river at a place called Johnsons Crossing. Sixty-five miles north of this Canol road, there lay a lake called Quiet, which was a number of things but quiet was not one of them. Early in the morning, if one was fortunate, one might find the water perfectly calm with a mirrorlike finish on the surface. By late morning, however, the winds began to blow, and noon brought whitecaps, which often remained late into the evening. This lake was at the head of a drainage system, which flowed through a succession of lakes connected by the Big Salmon River. The river traveled hundreds of miles through some of the most beautiful countries in the north then joined the Yukon River and flowed to the Bering Sea. Bob and Helen had studied maps for months, learning what they could about the valleys and plains, swamps and meadows that the river passed through. They had written for and received what information was available about the watershed. Hours were spent reading that data, studying, and making notes of such things as rapid locations, etc. Names of lakes and tributaries along the way were noted. Names of edible plants, animals, and mushrooms were recorded. It was to be a long trip, and canoes offered little room for provisions. Being able to supplement that diet with natural foods would certainly be a bonus.

They left Teslin early in the morning. A number of cottonlike clouds hung in the sky as the birds sang promises of a good day. Leaving the Alaska Highway, they turned north and started driving upward along the road that would lead them out of the Teslin River valley. The miles went by slowly as they followed along the ridge that would eventually lead to Quiet Lake and another valley, one that the Big Salmon River had taken years to carve out of the wilderness. They continued their way, passing lakes, crossing streams, stopping to admire the scenery and to enjoy the abundance of wildlife along the way. Bob continued to drive slowly, thankful for the solitude, scarcely able to contain himself. Several times since leaving the highway, he had voiced his complete approval with the words, "Helen, this is unbelievable!"

As they were approaching the lake, the road began descending. Catching glimpses of the water through the trees caused them both to smile in anticipation of the long-awaited canoeing holiday. They could not contain the happy feeling within themselves, which showed itself in the way they joked, laughed, and carried on like children. Joy continued to bubble from each of them as they drove up to the shore and stopped the car. For nearly an hour, they just sat, talked, and soaked up the beauty of it all. Looking up and down the lake, they scarcely could take it all in. It was now late afternoon, and the water was rough. They made camp, had a bite to eat, built a fire, and settled down to watch the sunset. The sun went down about midnight, sinking into a pink horizon, promising that tomorrow would be a good day. Bob and Helen climbed into their sleeping bags, cuddled up, and went to sleep. It had been a good day.

CHAPTER 4

B OB WOKE TO the smell of coffee. Helen was up and cheerfully starting breakfast. He got dressed and left the tent just as she began to fry the eggs. Picking up a cup, he poured himself some coffee and sat down to watch the performance. He did not grow up with a family of outdoor persons; though he often wanted to, he had never been camping before this trip. Helen had talked of her experiences in the wild and those good times she'd known as a child. It was her love of nature that sparked feelings hidden within Bob that had long lain dormant. As he sat on a log and watched Helen, he realized that he had never seen her as happy before. He was sure that she had missed her calling by becoming a teacher. She should have pursued a forestry career or something fish and wildlife related. However, she must surely have considered those things; who knows why we do what we do?

They enjoyed what was to be the last bacon-and-egg breakfast they'd have for some time. Eggs were just too bulky and fragile to be thrown in and out of a canoe morning and night, carried about all day with the rest of the gear and often pounded over white water. They just would not take the punishment, so they brought powdered eggs. From here on, eating was to be an experience, foreign to anything Bob had ever known. For the most part, staples were all the two would take; flour, salt, sugar, dried fruits, tea, powdered potatoes, and dry soup mixes made up a list of their stores. These would be supplemented with birds and small animals, fish, wild berries, natural edible roots, and mushrooms they'd find along the way.

After washing dishes and loading the canoe, the little bit of garbage they had was burned and then buried. They did not want to leave even a clue that they had passed this way; besides, the night before, they'd eaten canned vegetables for dinner, and the cans would decompose much better underground.

It was a team that struck out that morning so long ago, a good team. Not only were they man and wife—and God knows that marriage is no small feat—but they were much more than that; they were friends. As they struck out across the lake, they worked against one another for a short time. Soon, however, they began to paddle in a rhythm that carried them quickly over the water. This trip was not to be a test of strength and endurance; their plan was to paddle until they tired, then they'd stop, fish for a while, maybe build a fire, maybe not. In any case, they did not intend to spoil their honeymoon by overworking themselves. Paddling across the lakes would be hard work and slow progress as compared to drifting along with the current in the river. They allowed themselves plenty of time, however, and there certainly was no hurry. The two had felt certain that they'd witness much beauty on this trip, but neither of them was prepared for that first day and the wonders it brought to them. The waters were clear and cold, so the fish were firm and delicious. Never before had Bob been able to follow a fish's advance from the time it would see his lure until there was a strike and the fish was reeled in. He was like a child in the first grade on a nature hike; he just couldn't contain the grandeur of it all. Both Bob and Helen were enjoying themselves so much that they didn't realize how quickly night was creeping up on them. Evening found them still laughing and carrying on like children. Realizing that there would be no time to reach Big Salmon Lake, they headed for shore. They had planned to spend the night in a cozy log cabin, but now they'd have to camp on the beach.

It was a beautiful evening, the sun had gone down in a clear sky, and the moon was just beginning to show its light. A dead tree provided a ridgepole for their tarp, and as Helen prepared some things to eat, Bob put the finishing touches on what would serve as a tent. To conserve precious space, they had left their tent in the car, along with additional tarps and canned goods that were too bulky to carry in the canoe. After dinner was eaten and the dishes were washed, the two sat around the campfire, not wanting to go to sleep and miss any of the beauty. A loon called out from across the lake; a beaver swam close as if to announce his presence. He then slapped his tail and disappeared beneath the surface only to appear again a few hundred yards away. As the two climbed into their sleeping bags, they heard a grunting noise. Bob sat up quickly as if to say, "What was that!" Helen said, "Go to sleep, it's only a porcupine. It won't hurt you." He lay down once more, and soon, having been wearied by the events of the day, they both fell into a deep sleep. When Bob woke, Helen was sitting on a stump feeding a couple of camp robbers. The night before, she had fried fish for supper, and there had been some leftover. Bob quietly watched as the jays would fly down and land on her knee, then walk a few steps to take the meat from her hand. He wondered how long she'd sat there to gain their confidence and marveled at the lack of fear shown by these birds. After the offering was taken, the jays would fly off into the trees as if they were storing the food. When one left, the other would appear; they continued to alternate in this fashion until the fish was gone. Helen looked over at Bob, and he smiled back at her. His face lit up as a big grin showed undoubtedly that he approved of her actions and was somewhat fascinated by them. This second day out already was following closely on the heels of the first day. Awe-inspiring!

CHAPTER 5

W E OFTEN BECOME so involved with making a living that we neglect to enjoy life. This thought was running through Bob's mind that morning as they broke camp and prepared to continue their way. As they pointed the canoe out into the lake, shoved off, and established the paddling rhythm once again, he continued to daydream. A plan was beginning to take shape; his mind was playing games, but he was sure that they could make it work.

From the front of the canoe, Helen called out, "Here we go." They had reached the end of Quiet Lake, where the river runs out of the lake and immediately forms a rapid marked by shallow water and large jagged rocks, any of which would smash a canoe beyond recognition. In preparing for the trip, Bob and Helen had both become aware of the location and the seriousness of the white water. Bob was fully alert now, knowing how serious the situation was. The canoe began to speed up as the pull of the rapid sucked the water out of the lake; there was no turning back now. The shoreline whizzed by as Helen looked ahead and showed Bob where the deepest water was. There would be no problem if they could stay in the channel that had been cut out of solid rock over the years. Dodging fallen trees that stuck out into the streams and partially submerged boulders, they rode the current. Helen flashed signals, and Bob acted as a rudder, turning the canoe first this way and then that.

Downstream they sped, receiving scratches from the trees that hung out over the water. There were near misses, rocks that seemed to appear out of nowhere, deadheads and backwashes to be avoided. On they went as the minutes seemed like hours, down the river, tensed and alert, watching for the unexpected. As they proceeded, the water became increasingly shallow, and rounding a bend, the rapids stopped almost as quickly as they'd started. Bob and Helen had been so busy that they hadn't noticed the change in the landscape. They had passed a little bay, and now they were going by a swamplike area on one side and sheer rock face on the other. Bob, being scarcely able to take it all in, decided to anchor the canoe for a while and just gaze at the beauty of it all.

The canoe came to the end of the anchor rope in almost calm water. The river water was shallow and crystal clear, and arctic grayling swam lazily around the canoe as Bob and his wife sat amazed, almost close enough to reach out and touch them. Bob lifted his fishing rod and fastened a spinner to the end of the line. He cast the lure out into the deepest water, and almost before it hit the surface, he had a fight on his hands. Helen sat amazed, saying, "I can't let you get away with this," as she reached for her fishing rod. Bob continued to reel in his catch, and as the fish began to come close, it made one last lunge for freedom. The pull was enough to get Bob's attention; he knew he had hooked a good-sized fish. Bob repositioned himself, moving to a kneeling position so he could see into the water better, and when he did, he saw the giant grayling. He'd caught many grayling in his lifetime, fish of the three-quarter-to-one-pound variety, but never had he heard of one growing to be this size. The fish was well hooked; the only way it could escape was if Bob released it. When he took the lure, it was with a vengeance, and the hook was well set in his lip. Bob did release him though; there was no way that the two of them could eat a fish that big before it would begin to spoil. They were both fish lovers, but the grayling had weighed in excess of four pounds, too much even for them. The decision was made to tarry for a while longer, and many fish were caught and released from that one position in the river.

It was afternoon before the anchor was lifted, and they began once again to drift down the river. Having kept enough of the smaller grayling for a meal, they began to look for a site where they could build a fire and maybe enjoy an evening on shore once more. The valley with its beauty, silence, peaceful setting, and abundance of wildlife was generating a lasting effect on both Bob and Helen. Their friendship continued to grow as did their love for one another. They came to realize that they really needed very little besides one another and the many things which God had provided abundantly in this valley.

CHAPTER 6

THAT NIGHT WAS spent much as the first had been—under a tarp. They didn't wait for evening to fall before making camp, however. They came in off the lake early and went scouting. Following a creek bed, which wound its way through the trees, they arrived at a beaver dam. Having been there a long time, it now supported a growth of trees and grasses. The dam created a waterfall where the overflow tumbled over and fell into a pool beneath it. It was a perfect fishing spot, and bears had worn a path that led to it and away from it. This was not the safest place to be, they thought, but it was lovely. Returning to the lake, they stopped for a while and sat down. They stood at a place that was almost like a meadow. There was no growth except for the grasses that grew here and there. Thinking it very strange that trees would not grow in a place like this and looking at the map, they determined that this had to be Brown Creek. Then they looked across the creek and up the side of the mountain. The same condition existed far up the mountain, even beyond the tree line. It was as if a rock slide had come down and destroyed everything in its path. Then they realized that this was a slide area, not rocks but snow. On a sheer rock face like this, steep and long, the snow would build until its weight would bring it crashing to the valley floor. Neither Bob nor Helen liked the place, so they left. That night the wolves were howling, and Bob kept the campfire burning. In the wee hours of the morning, he was certain that he saw their silhouettes hugging the outer ring of light that shone from the campfire. Morning could not come soon enough, and as the first rays of light began creeping over the treetops, they loaded the canoe. Helen was in front and ready to push off before Bob had poured water on the fire. They went away from there with an eerie feeling and never looked back.

That morning they paddled harder than usual and continued to do so until they rounded a point and became separated from the sight of that creek. Upon doing that, the urgency seemed to fade, and once again they began taking more leisurely strokes. They continued to feel, however, that this lake was not a friendly place, and the sooner they could put it behind them, the better. As they continued their leisurely way, Bob decided to drag a spoon and see if he could catch a lake trout. It was hours before they reached the mouth of the river and left Sandy Lake behind them; in all that time, he didn't get one bite. When they entered the river, Bob made a comment. "You know, Helen, we didn't see one animal on that lake. Those wolves must have everything scared off."

"If we return, we'll follow the other shoreline and avoid Brown Creek."

That night was spent between Sandy Lake and Big Salmon Lake. They stopped early to prepare an early supper. Having skipped breakfast that morning and stopping early for lunch, by suppertime they were famished. Once they'd eaten and washed up, they began to explore the area once again. This time, there were no feelings of uneasiness as they had the previous evening. As it was still early, they followed the game trails and discovered some mineral springs, which were natural licks for the animals. As they drew closer to these licks, the trails all ran into one path cutting deep into the forest floor. Years of animal traffic to and from these locations left well-marked walkways. Roots that had once been nearly two feet below the ground were exposed now, creating small barriers the moose and caribou had to step over. These lay exposed to the weather and the animal traffic, beaten down and scarred by years of hooves and paws walking over and on them. They marveled at the sight and spoke of the possibilities a spot like this created—possibilities like that of watching the wildlife when they'd come here in the evening and an opportunity to pick and choose the proper individual game when hunting. This night they would climb the hill in back of this lick to a spot where they could set up a vigil and wait quietly for game to appear.

After sitting quietly for over an hour, they heard a twig snap, then suddenly a cow moose and her calf came into sight. They sniffed the wind carefully and then waded into the spring and drank deeply from the mineral water. Bob and Helen sat as though in a trance and watched the animals from their location. Being above the moose, their scent was carried off on the wind and undetectable to the animals. Darkness had fallen when the moose moved out of the pool, followed the path, and went on their way. It was late, and the trail back to the river was hard to follow, but soon they were nestled in their sleeping bags. They continued to discuss the event far into the night, mesmerized by the magnificence of it all. Visions of the animals were still on their minds when fatigue overtook them and they settled into deep sleep. Late morning arrived and found them still curled up in their bedrolls. It was Helen, once again, who woke first and sleepily walked to the river for water. The campfire was burning, and the water was almost boiling when Bob lifted his sleepy head.

It had been a long night of tossing and turning for Bob. Though he'd been tired, for some reason or other, sleep had eluded him. Between dreaming and lying awake, he had managed to get only a token amount of sleep. Opening his eyes in time to watch Helen chasing a squirrel first and then two camp robbers away from the grub box put him in a jovial mood. Laughing, he bounded out of bed and ran down to the creek to wash up.

During breakfast, clouds began to fill the sky, and by the time they packed up and pushed off to continue their journey, there were bolts of lightning flashing in the west. The storm continued to build as they entered the waters of the Big Salmon Lake.

The clouds blackened and hid the sun as the couple reached out their paddles, stretching forward and heaving back, desperate to reach the cabin that was supposed to be on this lake. Determined to do so before the clouds burst and the deluge struck, their muscles strained to achieve the task at hand. The clouds overhead boiled angrily as the lightning and thunder spurred them on.

The silhouette of the small cabin became visible, and Helen breathed a sigh of relief. "Thank goodness, preparation sources revealed the location of this cabin," she muttered. As they neared the point where the cabin stood, the storm broke. In seconds they were soaked to the skin; just a few more minutes and they'd have made it. They paddled up to the beach in front of the little log building and hurriedly carried their supplies inside. The tarp had kept everything dry, but in doing so, it had been soaked. It was taken inside and hung up to dry. The sleeping bags were laid out on the floor and opened up so the air could reach and dry any damp spots that might have resulted from the downpour. Only then did Bob return to the lake and pull the canoe farther up the beach. Laying two small logs on the sand, he turned the canoe over so that it rested upside down on the logs. He then returned to the cabin.

The lid on the airtight heater was popping, and the fire inside crackled when he opened the door. As the temperature began to rise inside the building, they removed their wet clothes and hung them up on a makeshift clothesline provided for such occasions. As they sat unclad in the dimly lit structure, their minds recounted the final minutes as they were approaching the cabin. They could now appreciate the humor of a situation that a short while ago had seemed to be so desperate. In truth, it could have been very desperate had a strong wind accompanied the thunder, lightning, and the rain. A canoe was not an ideal craft to be caught in when battling whitecaps and trying to stay afloat in rough water. Big Salmon Lake was a large body of water, and a brisk wind could cause all sorts of problems.

CHAPTER 7

THE RAIN CONTINUED to fall all through the night. The water formed puddles where it ran down to the beach and into the lake. All evening Bob had sat, talked, and listened as the rain fell on the tin roof and commented as to the hollow, soothing sound it produced inside the cabin. It was early when his eyes finally closed; he just lay back and fell asleep. Early in the morning, he woke and crawled into the warmth of his sleeping bag, then dropped off once more into a deep sleep. Hours later, unable to sleep any longer, Bob crawled out of bed; the downpour had slowed to a steady soaking drizzle. He was up early, the coffee pot was on the stove, and the bacon was frying in the small skillet they had brought along. He was pouring water into the powdered eggs with the intention of treating Helen to a breakfast in bed of bacon, scrambled eggs, and bannock when she opened her eyes. "My, aren't we energetic this morning," she said as she lifted her head from the homemade bed frame.

"Helen, I love it. I just can't get enough of this setting, and it's so peaceful. The silence is unbelievable. I'm even enjoying the rain. Can you believe that?" he said. Handing her a cup of coffee, Bob walked to the window and peered out. Plastic had been stretched over the window frame, and time had caused it to discolor and become brittle. He couldn't see much through it, but what he did see brought a smile to his face. A family of ducks had quietly approached, swimming slowly, floating and then disappearing beneath the surface of the lake. His attention having now been drawn to them, he could hear them quacking away to each other as though engaged in serious conversation. They didn't care that Bob was watching them as they continued their way, undaunted by the rain, which continued stubbornly to fall. He watched them until they rounded the point and went out of sight. Turning to look at Helen, he saw that she was in the process of finishing the job, preparing the breakfast that he had begun. He'd completely forgotten about it; if not for her, breakfast would have been burned to a crisp. They enjoyed having breakfast together that morning. They were content with their surroundings in spite of the rain, which refused to stop falling.

Bob had plenty of time to think about events that had led to his marrying Helen. In spite of their being so content together, he could not understand how two people so totally different could be so much alike.

They were two youngsters from completely different backgrounds, born into completely different lifestyles, and raised under different circumstances. They'd had nothing in common, nothing to build a relationship on, yet when they met, they found an instant communication link. Now they sat, a cup of coffee between them, giving thanks for the rain, for the ten-by-twelve-foot log cabin that kept them dry, for a love that continued to grow stronger with each passing day, and for being aware of the fact that they had been truly blessed. Noon brought a change in weather; the rain slowed to a sprinkle, and the sky began to show evidence of clearing. They were anticipating the resumption of their trip as the conditions slowly improved. Shortly after supper, they ventured outside once again. The lake had become calm, and raindrops were no longer breaking the surface of the water. A breeze began to blow about eight o'clock in the evening, a warm wind to dry the excess water that had collected on the trees and undergrowth and blow the remaining clouds from the sky.

The sun went down in a red sky and seemed to pull the colors with it as it disappeared over the treetops. Darkness fell over the valley, and the loons echoed their calls back and forth across the lake. Shortly the moon shed its light on the little cabin, and over the lake, the stars twinkled and promised the arrival of a pleasant new day. The fish began to jump in the bay, and as they broke the surface, a moonbeam glistened off the splash they'd made. Bob and Helen sat on the beach, enjoying it all. When the rain had stopped, they'd come outside and built a fire. They almost hated to go inside. As the night claimed more and more of the scenery and it became almost impossible to see anything at all, Bob extinguished the campfire, and hand in hand they headed for bed.

The beautiful red sunset of the previous night had truly resulted in an early-morning delight. As the sun rose over the horizon, it was a witness to the eagerness that Bob and Helen showed as they prepared for another day. The excitement of the moment allowed them time to wolf down toast and coffee. The anticipation of a pleasing day on the water spurred them on as they loaded the canoe. Just as the lake water began to feel the warmth of the sun and the mist was rising off the water, Bob pushed their craft away from shore, and another day had begun in the valley of the Big Salmon.

They hadn't gone far before seeing an island, a beautiful piece of land separated from the shore by a narrow channel of water. They couldn't continue without satisfying their curiosity, so the canoe was pointed toward shore. Reaching land was not easy because a shoal ran out from the island and the water was quite shallow. They did manage to dock, however, reaching land and stepping out of the canoe without as much as a wet foot. Immediately they realized that this location would provide a perfect camp spot. There was a natural opening cradled within a dense growth of trees on three sides. Two hundred feet or so from the beach, Bob climbed a hill that gradually ascended to overlook the entire area. Upon reaching the top, he looked at the terrain on the opposite side of the island and saw that it was much flatter and more exposed to the winds that would surely come blowing down the twenty miles of open water. This island was the first obstacle in the path of any such wind, and Bob shivered at the thought of how cold it would be there in the winter when the north wind would come howling down the expanse of ice and pile the snow in drifts on the flat land below. Now, however, there was no such wind, and the landscape was ominous but beautiful.

Sitting at the top of the ridge, Bob looked out and down at the whole of the island. It was lovely with its hill and meadowland, marsh and muskeg. It contained open spaces where a raw wind could cut a man to ribbons. It also had sheltered areas where somebody could build a small fire, put his back to a cliff, and comfortably wait out the worst of storms. He could see too that the sandy shoal ran all round the island. At the far end, it extended nearly a mile out into the lake. The marsh grass and cattails grew abundantly there, providing a variety of water plants that must have seemed like a smorgasbord to the moose population. Bob motioned to Helen, flashing signs and trying to make her understand that he wanted her to come up the hill and to bring his binoculars.

When she reached the top, he pointed toward the far end of the island, out past where the land stopped and the water began. Almost at the end of the shallow bar, just before the point where the lake water plunged to the depths, stood a cow moose with twin calves. They stood in the shallows, heads beneath the water's surface, feasting on the fresh shoots and the roots of the water plants. They were home here, far from the effects of man's world, living in their natural habitat with no thought of danger. They were concerned only with the task at hand, that of feeding and storing up fat, which was so necessary to carry these animals through the harsh northern winters. The cow had brought her calves out, knowing that there could be no safer place than this for them. It was a natural fortress for them. If any predators were to bother them, they'd just slip into the deep lake water and swim away. No animal swam as fast, as far, and as long as the moose could. An air pocket inside each individual hair provided the animal with ideal buoyancy and enabled it to remain in the water almost indefinitely, certainly long enough to outlast any predator. The big cow, having two calves, was using all the instinct she was born with to protect her family. Almost any other location imaginable would provide less security in the event of a wolf attack. One calf, in such circumstances, would be difficult to defend. To save them both under these conditions would be impossible. The cow would stay here all summer while her calves grew. They'd have an abundance of food and constant supply of water, and safety was just a jump away in the deep waters of the lake. Bob and Helen watched them a while longer, very much impressed by it all, marveling at the way nature does provide for her creatures. They slowly walked to the canoe leaving the hill between them and the beauty that lay beyond it.

As they pushed themselves out into the deep water once more, Bob looked at Helen and said, "I'd like to come back here one day. We could spend a couple of days down in that meadow just looking and fishing the deep water just off that paddy where the moose were." She made a mental note of the words he was saying and nodded in complete agreement.

CHAPTER 8

LOOKING AHEAD, BOB studied the shoreline, and it appeared as though they had reached the end of the lake. They contemplated turning and heading straight north toward the outlet to the river. They decided instead to spend the remainder of that day sightseeing, assuring themselves that they had indeed seen everything that was available there.

Helen called to Bob and pointed skyward. Some Canada geese were approaching, flying low and straight. Hoping that they would come closer, Bob sat motionless, paddle across his knees; Helen followed suit. The birds flew over the canoe and disappeared into what up to then had appeared to be the timberline. Two very surprised people began paddling hard, straining themselves in an effort to reach the point quickly. Soon the canoe approached a point of land that extended out into the water, a peninsula that had hidden an impressive body of water from their sight. As they entered the sheltered bay, it soon became apparent that this was not just any ordinary, run-of-the-mill inlet; it was a veritable bird sanctuary. As the canoe slowly moved along close to shore, some of the birds seemed to make a game of coming close, then diving only to appear a few feet away.

There were birds there that they had never seen before, and of course, many that they had. They enjoyed trying to identify them as they flew by or swam lazily with their young ones. There were four different species of geese, mallards, pintails, teals, and others. They saw grebes, loons, herons, cranes, and many others. Even the numbers of land birds were impressive; among them were bald eagles, falcons, hawks, and an osprey. They even flushed a grouse from cover when they went ashore to camp for the night, and to think they'd almost not discovered the passage to this apparent paradise for birds.

It was obvious to both Bob and Helen that there was plenty of food in this cove for their newfound feathered friends, but still their curiosity got the best of them. All evening they'd either swim or fly to the edge of the campsite, begging for handouts and receiving them. As the canoe would slip through the water during the course of the day, Bob dragged a fishing line and lure. He caught a number of small lake trout, a few of which he kept. When the birds began their begging, Helen fried a few more than were needed for supper, and she and Bob spent hours playfully teasing their new friends with the excess fried fish.

As the days went by, they became more and more attached to the valley and especially to this lake. They became reluctant to leave, even though realizing that far more time had been spent here than had been originally planned.

The sun was high in the sky when they finally broke camp and moved on down the lake. Sadness was evident as they paddled through the narrow channel that led back to the large body of lake water. "Surely someday we'll return here," Bob said as he pulled hard on his paddle, and the canoe moved on down the lake. It was late July when they approached the end of Big Salmon Lake. Many days had been spent there camping, fishing, and just spending the time that was needed to understand each other and to grow close. They didn't care much that a month had almost passed since leaving home. They were concerned more that time was running short and soon they'd have to leave the lake, an area that had quickly begun to feel like home and was becoming a part of each of them.

CHAPTER 9

THAT EVENING, AFTER camp was set up, they walked down to the river that ran out of the lake. They noticed a different type of fish moving through the water. These were reddish in color and much larger than they'd seen so far. Their research on the area had not revealed to them that these were salmon. There were only a few present at that time, but within a few days, the river bottom would run red, alive with king salmon. Once a year they came up river to spawn, making sure that there would always be a yearly trek of these fish from salt water to fresh.

Bob and Helen had no way of knowing then that it was a mistake to camp so close to this spot during the salmon run. They were not familiar with the procedure that was to take place this time of year as it had done so for hundreds of years.

They set up camp for the night on the shore of the lake, close enough to the river outlet to hear the water gurgling over the rocks; they began to prepare their evening meal. As the campfire began to roar, the smell of pine smoke drifted through the trees. It was carried by the light breeze out over the water of the river and continued downstream a good distance before it disappeared. It had been a long tiresome day, and both Bob and Helen were quite hungry. As the meal she was preparing began to cook, the aroma it produced was also carried slowly down the river. The fire got hotter and produced less smoke, but the smell of food became stronger and stronger and continued to reach out and cover the area. While the meal cooked, Bob and his wife sat talking and enjoying a cup of tea. They were discussing the many things that had taken place in the last few days, things that would be remembered always.

As they sat within the rim of light produced by the fire, they had no way of knowing that the smells being scattered by the breeze had not gone unnoticed. It was making his yearly journey toward the fishing spot that he knew so well. As he came closer, the smells told him that all was not well; something had changed. He was not impressed that there were intruders in his territory; he would not allow it. The smells became stronger, and the grizzly bear stood up, sniffed the wind again, and looked the area over. He was a magnificent animal who stood a full nine feet. His coat glistened; the black on his back faded to dark brown when nearing his upper legs, then changing to a lighter brown as his coat extended down to his paws. His massive shoulders were almost white in color. He was a beautiful sight to see as he stood in the twilight, a full-grown adult silvertip. He was very close to the source of strange smells he had been following, so close that had Bob known, he'd have packed everything and left the area.

When the grizzly stopped at the tree line a short distance from camp, Bob was just finishing the last of his bannock. Helen had begun to wash the dishes and stood facing down the beach, looking in the bear's direction. She saw the bear move out of the trees and stand erect, pawing the air and swinging his head from side to side. Slowly he dropped back down to all fours and began to approach. Helen, having grown up in the wild, knew that the worst possible thing to do was panic. When she first noticed the bear, she stopped doing the dishes and slowly walked toward the canoe. It had been dragged up to the beach with everything still in it except for the grub box. Helen had the canoe in the water before Bob realized there was something wrong. Helen pointed up the beach, and Bob followed the point. The bear roared and stood up once more, not being sure as to what he should do next. The scent that was coming to him was something he'd never smelled before, nor had he seen this type of animal before. The strange animal was a mystery to him, and because of that, he was unsure as to what he should do.

The bear's indecision had given Helen the needed time to get the canoe into the water. She whispered to Bob to pick up the grub box and get in the canoe. The sound of her voice seemed to snap the grizzly out of the trance he'd been in, and once again he began to approach with confidence. Bob had the supplies in the canoe and stood in water up to his knees when the big bear began to lope toward them. Bob got into the canoe and shoved off, heaving on his paddle in an effort to put more water between them and the bear. As the canoe struck straight out toward the middle of the lake, the bear came running down the beach in knee-high water. He came on the run, growling, teeth bared, water flying from his feet. The animal was no longer undecided; he knew now what he would do. If he could catch the strange animals, he would make sure that they'd never again enter his territory. Bob and Helen were fortunate; they'd escaped. Due to experience, Helen had not panicked; she'd remained calm and made the best of a bad situation. They had come away with most of their possessions but not all.

At sunrise they returned to reclaim their possessions and found that the bear had really done a number on their camp. Their tarp had been completely ruined, ripped to shreds by tooth and claw. The dishpan was mangled by the animal and then, along with the dishes that had been in it, was buried in the sand. Bob salvaged the dishes, but their tarp shelter and dishpan were totally useless. They were now forced to make what was, for them, a very difficult decision.

To continue the trip without shelter from the rain would not be realistic. The tarp had been more than adequate to keep the rain off and their body heat in when sleeping. It was gone now, and so too was any opportunity to continue downstream. The river would just have to wait until a future date when opportunity would once again present itself, and they could continue. For the present, Bob decided that they would continue back upstream to where they'd begun the trip. There was the matter of some remaining vacation time, however, and they planned to spend all the time in the area. Leaving the bear scare behind, they began looking for a suitable site where they could spend the afternoon, but first they'd have lunch.

CHAPTER 10

A S THE EVENING progressed and the moon began to cast its light onto the lake, Bob and Helen pulled the canoe up in front of the log cabin. They had returned here knowing from the previous experience with the rainstorm that the building was sound and would provide needed refuge from the elements. Having enjoyed themselves here during that storm, they decided to spend a few more days now that weather conditions had improved.

Because of the previous foul weather, they had not noticed a game trail behind the cabin. The trail began behind the cabin, continued into the trees, extended over the hill, and ran for miles. Through draws, over ridges and creeks, it traversed a large area and opened it up to the enjoyment of those who were avid hikers.

Bob and Helen started up the path the following morning. After preparing a pack that would enable them to remain overnight, they went up the hill from the small cabin and disappeared from view. Equipped with fishing rods and a box of fly hooks, they walked gingerly along the path. They, of course, had not been there before, but surely they'd find a beaver dam or a waterfall, they thought. As the day wore on and a panorama of beauty lay before them, they almost forgot about fishing. Spending hours just sitting and marveling at the lovely scenery, they remained awed by the grandeur of it all.

The remainder of the day was spent sitting and dreaming among the flowers and whiling away the hours, attempting to name the different plants and determining which were edible and which were not. When they reached the first small creek, they decided to stop and camp. It was early afternoon when Helen put a stew on to cook, and it sat bubbling away for hours. Bob followed the creek downstream to try and find a fishing spot but returned shortly without fish and short of breath. That night, just as darkness settled over the area, they heard footsteps a short distance away. A twig snapped, and two moose came into view and stood on the path. They stopped suddenly; seeing Bob and Helen had surprised them, and they stood dazed for a moment, not knowing what to do. Then they bolted, left the path, and ran down through the trees. Noisily they ran through the underbrush for a short distance, and then it was quiet once again, and they were gone. The squirrels noisily signaled their departure to their neighbors and then quietly resumed their curious spying tactics. They scurried to and fro, keeping a watchful eye on their new neighbors. They neither cared for nor trusted these individuals to whom they were unaccustomed. The little animals were not about to rest until Bob and Helen left. The night passed without further incident, and Bob slept soundly as did Helen.

They woke early, fully refreshed and ready for another day. The air was cooler that morning than they had remembered, and clouds began to appear in the sky. A breeze began to blow, and from where they stood, high on a ridge above the valley, it began to feel very much like snow. They hurriedly gathered their belongings and started to return to the cabin. As Bob threw his backpack, a few drops of rain fell. A brisk walk was just what they needed to warm themselves up, and two hours later, they had descended to a lower elevation, and the rain had stopped. It was warmer now, but the dark clouds continued to fill the sky and make promises of a heavy downpour.

Shortly after reaching the cabin, Bob started a fire, and as the heat began to fill the building, the rain began to fall. They had expected a heavy rain but received a light soaking shower all night. Early morning brought no letup. Bob went outside to bring in some wood for the fire and studied the sky. There was no evidence that the storm would break soon. The clouds were black and thick; there were no breaks where the sun might try to shine through. Early afternoon found Helen rolling out dough on the cabin table. She was making a few biscuits for breakfast, certain that they would have to remain here until at least the following morning. Sitting outside the door under the overhanging roof of the cabin, Bob embarked on playing a game with a chipmunk. The tiny animal appeared to be making his home underneath the floorboards. Bob noticed that the little rodent was carrying seeds and storing them for the approaching winter months. He quite enjoyed watching the performance. Cheek pouches full, the chipmunk would disappear beneath the cabin only to appear once again with pouches empty. Off he'd go into the underbrush, soon to return with another pouch full, which he also stored. Helen heard Bob chuckling to himself, and curiosity got the better of her, so out she came to see what was going on. When Helen opened the door, she saw Bob tossing tiny pieces

SID BELL

of dried fruit to the far side of the cabin. He motioned for her to sit down. She did so quietly, and soon the chipmunk appeared once more, loaded the fruit into his pouches, and again disappeared to store the treasure.

Evening came to the valley and brought with it the first signs that maybe the sky would clear and the rain stop. Shortly after midnight, the rain did quit falling, but when morning came, the cloud cover still hung over the lake. It was noon before the sky attempted to clear; a few rays of sunshine began to show themselves as a breeze started to blow. Soon an odd small cloud could be seen overhead, but for the most part, the sky was clear once again. For the balance of the day, Bob put the canoe in the water and went fishing. Two days had passed since they last had fish for supper, and he was craving a feed of lake trout. He was fortunate; fish tend to bite well after a rainfall, and he caught some nice ones. Bob returned shortly before supper with the few fish he'd kept. He walked up to the cabin and handed them to Helen; all were cleaned and ready for the frying pan. As she removed their heads and placed them in the pan, she checked the other dishes she'd been preparing. Supper was soon ready, and as they sat and ate their meal, they talked about what they'd do the following day. The sun slipped over the horizon as Helen poured another cup of coffee. Far into the night they were still sitting at the table making plans.

CHAPTER 11

I T WOULD TAKE two days to reach Quiet Lake; two days of continuous hard work paddling against the current would be slow. There were locations where the rapids were so strong that a portage would be necessary. All the details had been previously discussed; they were well aware that this portion of the trip would not be easy. It was necessary, however, and they were determined to make a success of it. Sometime after midnight, they decided that they should retire for the night. A full day lay ahead of them; they'd have to be well rested to bring it to a successful close.

When Bob and Helen got started the following morning, it was later than they'd planned on. The sun was well up over the treetops, and the mist had risen from the water when they started across the lake. As if hating to leave, they took one last look at the cabin and then went to work with their paddles. When far out from shore, they turned once more, and a permanent picture became etched on their minds—a picture of the beauty that lay before them. They had fully enjoyed their stay, and Lord willing, they'd be back.

As they once again began to paddle, the canoe slipped silently through the water, a witness to the sadness that rode with them. The deepest feelings are always shown in silence. So it was that morning as they continued to paddle, making their way across the expanse of water. Quietly they went about their task, each of them thinking, reflecting in their own way on the various aspects that had so endeared this country to them. They had come to care deeply for the north during the weeks they had spent there. With the sadness that they each felt now that they had to leave, there was also happiness. They were content in the knowledge that after all the planning, they had seen at least a portion of the beauty that this valley had to offer. Hopefully, someday, there would be a time to see the rest. Feeling sure that there would be a return visit, for the present they'd cling to that hope.

Off in the distance, Helen could see the mouth of the river; she looked back at Bob and pointed ahead. "The easy part's over," she said. "Now the hard part begins." They had been skimming along quite well up to that point where the idle lake water offered very little resistance to their effort. Both effort and resistance were multiplied once the canoe entered the river. The progress slowed considerably, and to make headway at all, they found that working together was most important. They struggled and strained to gain the distance needed to reach the quiet water that lay at the head of each rapid. From a kneeling position, both Bob and Helen reached forward and plunged the paddle deep, pulling hard. Beads of perspiration formed on their foreheads and ran down into their eyes, continuing down their faces; the beads grew larger and dripped from their chins, mixing with the river water. On went their struggle, and slowly they gained the precious feet that were needed. When reaching the quieter water, they'd hold on to trees that extended out into the stream. In this way they'd anchor themselves and hold their position while they rested, catching their breath and preparing themselves to continue. Within minutes they'd be off again, up river to the next rapid where the river once again entered into conflict with their determination. Despite the hard work and the slow progress, they were steadily inching their way upstream. Patience grew thin as muscles became sore, and Helen decided that it was time for lunch and a strong cup of coffee. Bob seconded the motion.

They pulled the canoe onto the rocky shore, and Bob went searching for dry driftwood to make a fire. Helen sat down on a flat rock, leaned against a root, and fell fast asleep though she had not intended to do so. When Bob returned, he started a fire and set the coffee pot on a rock beside it. Soon the flames had heated the water to a boil. As the water bubbled over the coffee grounds, an aroma was released that began to carry toward Helen. As the smell of coffee filled the air, Helen awoke with a start and couldn't believe how fast she'd conked out. Reaching for a cup, she poured herself some coffee. The feeling slowly returned to her hands, but they continued to ache from the effect of the cold water. Her knees were sore as well; the strain that had been put on them had certainly left an impression. They'd been chaffed to the point where they were now red, and in two places, the skin had even been rubbed until raw. *There must be a better way*, she said to herself. At the same time she was thinking, *This coffee sure tastes good.*

Bob spoke up, "We've got to get going, dear, if we're going to reach Sandy Lake before nightfall." Off they went once again though Helen was very reluctant at first and came close to suggesting that they stay and camp there on the riverbank for the night.

Helen thought again about the condition of her knees and decided that she would not paddle from a kneeling position when they reached the next rapid. She'd work instead from a sitting stance, thereby relieving the pain she knew kneeling would bring. It was not long before they reached another rapid and Helen had an opportunity to test the plan she'd made earlier. Helen found that she could neither navigate properly from a sitting position nor get much thrust into each stroke of the paddle. It soon became evident that once again she would have to kneel if they were to make any headway at all. Again she began to work, resting on sore knees, and once again the pain returned. When they reached the top of the rapid, Bob could see that Helen was having a tough time. "What would you say if I told you we just passed the last of the fast water between here and Sandy Lake? The next rapid we'll come to is the bad one near Quiet Lake," he said.

"I'd say that I hope you are right," Helen replied.

He was right! The paddling became much easier, and even though Helen's knees had been rubbed raw and were very sore, she was glad that she and Bob had not stopped to camp earlier. It was a relief to sit back and stretch her legs while Bob did most of the paddling. Once more they began to enjoy the trip as they moved slowly along. Bends in the river came and went; first, one type of animal was sighted, then another as the couple made their way up the stream, coming ever closer to Sandy Lake. They had made plans to camp overnight on the lake and get an early-morning start, their intention being to complete the last leg of the trip back to the car that they'd left at Quiet campsite. Well before sunset, the canoe floated around a curve in the river; looking ahead, Helen could see the widening of the water where the river entered the lake. "We've arrived," she said. "For a while there, I really had doubts." It had been a tiresome day; they both were exhausted and sore. As they pulled the canoe up onto the sandy lakeshore, Bob could think of only two things: food and sleep. Not necessarily in that order.

CHAPTER 12

A S A NEW day broke, the sun cast its rays through the trees that stood high on the ridge. These rays of light, swept in bars and filtered by the mist, cast shadows on the surface of the water. Out of the mist appeared a canoe. Bob and Helen had been awakened by the loons calling back and forth across the lake's expanse and signaling to all that a new day had dawned in the valley. They now moved in and out of the shadows cast by the sun as it shone on the rising vapor that still hung over the lake. They had retired early due to the exhaustion of a hard day. A fish jumped as the mist continued to rise slowly from the surface of the water. Encouraged by this, Bob dropped a lure over the side of the canoe; maybe there'd be fish for supper. As he reached to grab the paddle once more, he grimaced a bit. Both he and Helen were slow to move around that morning, even though they had put a few miles of water behind them and the night's campsite; they were still stiff and sore. Surely the combination of the sun's warmth and the resumption of paddling would be enough to work out the stiffness, they thought. Slowly their muscles began to limber up, and as the hours went by, they felt increasingly better.

Bob had decided to follow along the east shore of the lake this time. When they had first come here, they'd hugged the west shore, camped on Brown Creek, and had a bad experience there. The eerie feeling that the encounter had produced had left him with a bad impression. If the events of the day went according to plan, there would be no need to camp on the lake again. Bob hoped that nightfall would find them far up the river from the shores of Sandy Lake. He was quietly thinking about that situation as he continued to paddle the canoe, following a rhythm he'd become accustomed to during the last few weeks. When the tip of his fishing rod began to twitch, his daydream ended. The rod bent almost in half, and his reel began to sing as the fish ran the line out. "Maybe there's some hope for this lake after all," he said as the fish continued to fight. When the line went slack, Bob felt that it had broken and his prize had escaped. Then he felt another tug, and his lure was pulled to the depths. It went slack again, and Bob realized that the trout was coming, once again, to the surface. He reeled his line in quickly in an effort to catch up with the fish. No sooner did he tighten up on the line once more than down the trout would go again and the reel would sing once more.

Forty minutes later, Bob was still trying to outguess the creature. Because of the light tackle he was using, he could not do anything but take his time, play with the fish, and hope he'd tire himself out. Helen was certain that Bob had hooked a big one, and it certainly felt that way to him. So on went the cat-and-mouse game until finally the trout was pulled alongside the boat. They used the net to lift him into the canoe; one flop and the fish would have been back in the lake. When lifting him into the boat, the hook fell out of his mouth; another minute and he'd have been gone. Bob had never seen a trout that large; completely played out, he just lay half in and half out of the net. Never so much as an effort was made to escape until he reached the bottom of the canoe. The hook was removed from the net; the fish was held in the water for a while until he began to breathe again. One flip of his tail and he was gone, all twenty seven pounds of him.

Again the two vacationers continued their way. Bob continued to smile as they neared the mouth of the river once more, still very much contented with himself over the prize catch. Soon they would reach rough water and the smile would be gone, but for now, he'd think of that fish over and over. It had been a beauty.

They stopped for a while when they reached the point where the gravel bottom began. The water here was shallow and moved quickly over the rocks. Better grayling fishing could not be found, and they planned on having fish for supper. Bob and Helen both were wishing they had days to spend here instead of just hours, for they thoroughly enjoyed the experience. Many fish were caught; a few were kept as the afternoon wore on. Time, being one of man's greatest enemies, once again determined that they move on.

The anchor was pulled into the canoe, and they continued their upstream quest. They wanted to reach the outlet from Quiet Lake before nightfall and spend the night on the shore with the rapids behind them. When they rounded a bend in the river, the current quickly became stronger. Try as they would, they could not make any headway against the current. When lifting their paddles to make another stroke, they'd lose the momentum they'd gained the time before. The current was becoming so strong that it was foolish to continue. Bob decided they'd go to shore and unload the canoe. There was a game trail that followed the river, a good path made by years of animal travel. He'd use his backpack to carry the supplies and bedrolls, and he and Helen would portage this rapid. The sun had almost set before the lake was sighted. The trek up the riverbank had almost demanded more than they had to give, but the lake came into sight, and with it came new hope. Now that the end was near, they dug deep and found some strength that had been held in reserve. When they reached the lake, their muscles were almost too sore to lower the canoe from their backs. As soon as they lay the canoe on the sand, they dropped to their knees and rested awhile. Helen was all for going to sleep right there, but the wind was beginning to blow, and Bob knew that they'd have more protection on the opposite shore. He asked her if she could hang together until they could cross over to a spot where they'd have shelter and a good supply of firewood.

That night it rained! They were just finished eating when they felt the first drops. Despair was about to set in when Helen got an idea. After explaining it to Bob, the two of them went to work and cut a number of spruce boughs. They made a bed of these boughs and stretched their sleeping bags out on top of them. Then they crawled into their bags and pulled the canoe over themselves. The canoe sitting upside down high on the beach was all that could be seen. Bob and Helen were up on the spruce boughs away from the wet ground and under the canoe away from the rain. They slept dry and they slept long; the events of the day had left them completely worn out. The wind continued to blow, and the rain fell heavily far into the night. The huge drops bounced off the craft and echoed inside as the wind whistled and whitecaps rose on the lake. The waves pounded the shore, reaching a point that was well up the beach, breaking near the canoe and then returning to rise again. The lightning flashed and thunder roared, but Bob and Helen slept on. The water collected in pools on the beach and then overflowed to form little streams as they ran to the lake. A loom swam up to the edge of their camp and called out, yet on they slept.

When finally they woke and rolled the canoe off themselves, the rain had stopped, and the sky was beginning to clear. Bob sat up and rubbed the sleep from his eyes then pulled his pants on and headed for the trees. When he returned, Helen was busy trying to find some wood that was dry enough to burn. Bob dropped a bundle of sticks and dried moss onto the spruce boughs. He'd gone and broken some dead twigs from the pine trees. These sticks, sheltered as they are, remained dry in the worst of rainstorms.

Coupled with the moss he'd also taken from the trees, it was not long until a fire was blazing away. "You could become quite good at this outdoor living if we keep it up," she said. She thought of how well Bob had adapted to this way of living and smiled. Not only was he competent, but also he really enjoyed it, and that was a bonus.

When they'd finished eating breakfast, the lake was completely calm. It almost seemed a shame to launch the canoe and rile the surface. Launch it they did, however, and shortly before noon, they began the last leg of the journey. They remained quiet as the distance between them and the car quickly shortened. They'd almost come to the end of their honeymoon vacation. It had been both a joy and an education. These weeks had brought them closer to one another. They had each learned many things about their partner, important things, things that had drawn them closer. They learned of their character strengths and weaknesses, of how to communicate more fully, of deeper respect and trust. They learned too of strong convictions they held, of little things that brought laughter, others that could bring tears. *Yes!* They had learned many things, and they were sorry that this experience was coming to a close. Soon they would reach the campsite where they had left their vehicle.

CHAPTER 13

T HE CAR WOULD, once again, link them with the smoke and the smog of the city. The city brought to mind the traffic jams, the tension, the vanity of the almighty dollar. They had spent their lives preparing to take their place alongside all the others who were so involved in making a living and left little time to make a life. They had been there and were not looking forward to going back. After the beauty that they'd known during the preceding weeks, they couldn't bring themselves to rejoice over returning to the concrete jungle. The silence continued until they reached the car; only then was it broken. Bob stepped out into the cold water. "Can't put it off any longer, hon," he said. "We've arrived."

After pulling the canoe through the shallow water and up onto the beach, he quickly took off his shoes and socks. "How can that water stay so cold all summer?" he said. Helen went about the task of preparing a lunch while Bob built a fire and dried his footwear.

Bob drove down the road a short distance. It followed the lakeshore for a few miles and offered a number of campsites that were practically on the water. He continued, however, stopping after reaching one he'd noticed when they had first arrived here six weeks earlier. It was set back in the trees, sheltered from the open water. That morning the sun had risen in a red sky, and he was expecting the lake to get rough. It was almost noon when he drove the car up to the fire pit. Taking a tarp out of the trunk, he stretched it vertically between two trees. The tarp formed a wall on the southwest side of their camp and provided an efficient windbreak. Bob then lit the fire and walked down to the lake with his fishing rod. He stood thinking, casting out his line, and reeling it back in. It was not long before the wind began to blow. Bob shivered as the blast seemed to almost penetrate clear through to his bones. He walked back to the trunk of the car, unwrapped, and strung another tarp. The heat from the fire ricocheted off the tarps and back toward the center of the enclosure. He and Helen sat within this makeshift shelter and remained as warm as toast. That night they'd planned to have a feast and began preparing for it. Much of the food they'd brought for the trip had been left in the car's trunk, bulky things that they couldn't take down the river. Now that they had returned, they could once again utilize all these. An abundance of canned goods, potatoes, different meat stews, vegetables, and seafood were some of what they had to choose from. As Helen busied herself with the preparations for the meal, Bob settled back against a tree, sitting on a log, and recalled events as they'd unfolded over the course of the trip.

Late afternoon brought gale force winds, and three-foot whitecaps pounded the beach. As the evening wore on, there were no signs that the storm might end anytime soon. Bob remained in comfort within the walls that the tarps provided. He and Helen were quite content, cozy, and warmly nestled in their refuge. Suppertime came, and the meal Helen had prepared was eaten and thoroughly enjoyed. Bedtime brought cloudy skies; the wind changed and blew from the northwest, and rain began to fall. Bob lay awake for quite some time listening to the ringing of the rain as it pounded on the roof of the car. He was reluctant to fall asleep, knowing that this would be the last night they'd spend in the valley for some time.

Life sometimes plays hardball, throwing us curves, sliders, and we find ourselves questioning the umpire. There comes a time in all our lives, he thought, *when we should stop taking things so seriously. If we could put down our tools, walk out into an open field, lie down and smell the flowers, learn to enjoy the little things, then we could see more clearly which things are really important.* He planned, then, to never let the task of making a living so cloud his thinking as to forget that when God gave us life, he promised that if we live according to his will, we can also have contentment. As Bob slowly slipped into a deep sleep, he was thinking of how contented he could be if he lived in this valley.

Daylight broke on a chilly day in August about seventy-five miles north of the sixtieth parallel. The rain had stopped falling, but the wind continued to blow. The sky remained dark, and it was obvious that the situation would get worse before it improved. Thankful that the rain had stopped, Bob began to break camp. He picked up the few things that had been left out in the rain, folded the tarps, and put them in the trunk. He then checked the canoe tie-downs to ensure that they had remained tight. Helen was awake and had the coffee pot perking by the fire. She and Bob talked, drinking until the pot was empty, then went to the lake, rinsed the pot, poured water on the fire, and departed.

SID BELL

CHAPTER 14

THE TRIP HOME was uneventful. They drove for five days, starting early and retiring early. During those days, they went on about the beauty of the valley. Again and again they relived the events, and one of the many things that they continued to agree upon was the fact that they would certainly return. They had not expected to enjoy themselves the way they had, and they did not want to leave. Even the bear scare would be fondly remembered, if not as a joy, then certainly as an education. A shiver overtook Helen as she remembered the beast coming down the beach, running in the shallows, water splashing, a growling in his throat, and destruction on his mind. A few more minutes and they'd have been done for, but they'd been given those minutes. She smiled and was content.

It was late when they arrived, so Bob decided that he'd unpack the car in the morning. He went inside the house and upstairs to the bathroom off the master bedroom and had a shower. Helen had stopped at the downstairs bath and poured the water. They whistled and sang for nearly a half hour, enjoying the warm water. Over the preceding six weeks, they had bathed in northern waters that could be well described by only one word: *cold*. A quick dip was necessary to get themselves wet, then they'd run up onto the beach to soap themselves up. That completed, they'd run into the water once more to wash the soap off. A dip and a quick rub of the hair and then back to the beach where they'd stand in the sun and shiver until dry. Bob thought for a second then said aloud, "This is one nice thing about living in the city."

In the morning, after the car was unloaded and the tarps were hung up to air out, Bob phoned his parents, and they came for coffee. The rest of that day was spent explaining, and Bob was more than willing to explain the details to them. Helen too gave quite a descriptive picture of some of the circumstances, and soon Mom and Dad were wishing they could have been there. Less than a week had elapsed since they left the lake when already Bob began missing the valley, the good fishing, the clear water, the peaceful existence, and the cabin. There would always be that cabin. He thought long, in the days that followed, about his valley, the river, and the lakes; but mostly his mind reflected images of Big Salmon Lake. There was the cabin and the natural bird sanctuary, the island moose nursery, the natural mineral licks, and the salmon run, not to mention the terrific fishing. It seemed to Bob that all the things a man needed were on or near the lake. It was such a lovely spot.

Just a few vacation days remained for Bob. Shortly he would have to return to the screaming saws, pounding hammers, and the constant pressure to finish a job only to begin another and repeat the performance. He curled up on the couch with a good book and became lost, once again, in the wilderness. Bob was dreading the thought of returning to the workplace. It was not the work so much that he minded; it was the never-ending demand that the system had put on him and others. It seemed to Bob that he was working long hard hours and getting nowhere. Even the home they lived in had been left to Helen when her father passed on. By the time the bills were paid, there was nothing left. Income tax, property tax, car payments, insurance costs, fuel and upkeep expenses, carpenter tools he needed, utility bills, and other expenses left very little money for themselves. Had they been buying a home instead of owning one, thanks to Helen's dad, there'd have been a shortage. Bob was becoming less and less enthused with city life and all the expenses that went with it. Regardless of how hard he worked, it seemed that at best he could only remain in the same situation. He would be content, for the present, to go on playing the game, being certain that an opportunity would present itself and a way would be shown to him, a way of escape from this trap. It reminded him of a hamster wheel in a hamster's cage. Around and around the wheel would spin, but the animal would remain in the same place. What a fool the hamster is, some might think, but he cannot get out of his cage. In order to continue living, he must eat and exercise to sustain his good health. Like the hamster, Bob was in a cage and couldn't find a way out. The city was Bob's cage, and the system was the tread wheel. He'd continue to work, and the tread wheel would continue to impede any progress. Unlike the hamster though, Bob would go on looking for a way out of his cage, and he felt certain that the way would be found eventually.

CHAPTER 15

O N A MONDAY morning late in August, Bob rose early, went to the window, and looked out. The sun was shining brightly somewhere that morning, but from where he stood, only its outline could be seen. Try as it did, the sun could not penetrate the smog that hung in the air. Walking back to the bed and sitting down, he pulled his socks on. Normally Bob was a bundle of energy, but since returning home, he'd been in a state of semidepression. He needed to return to the normal routine of living and set aside his hope of escape for the present. Surely once he was back on the job, the discontentment would leave him. He knew that there would always be the yearning for a simpler lifestyle, but to pine for it the way he was doing couldn't be healthy. When he'd finished dressing, he began to shave as the smells of breakfast floated into the bathroom. Helen was up and had the coffee brewing. In spite of the fact that Bob had been testy during the last few days, she remained happy. As he continued to get ready for work, unimpressed as he was, the sound of her singing floated through the house, a testimony to the love that remained so much a part of her. Bob smiled in spite of himself and spoke out so that she could hear him, "What did I ever do to deserve you? Helen, you could bring a smile to the lips of a dying man if only he could be a witness to your overcoming attitude." Bob knew of course that he had done nothing that entitled him to her love. Helen was a gift, and he was well aware of her value. She was very much needed and appreciated and had become a friend he could no longer go on without.

Bob ate breakfast, then walked outside and started the car. Helen followed. Bending down, she kissed him good-bye. Before he drove off, however, she said, "I have an appointment to see the doctor today. I've had some headaches and nausea lately, and it's been a while since I've had a checkup. I'll tell you all about it when you get home."

Bob went to work, and as much as he'd imagined, the worst was over once he began; it had been a long vacation, maybe too long. It was hard to return to the drudgery of eight to five, day in and day out, five days a week. The alternative remained much more to his liking: coming and going as he liked, getting out of bed when he woke, fishing, camping, hiking, and telling stories. I suppose though, if there were no bad times we wouldn't recognize the good. The day unfolded quickly as he threw himself into his work. Boredom cannot take hold of a worker who remains determined to get the job done. Bob found that the harder he worked, the less he'd think about the vanity of his lifestyle. At the end of the day, he had beaten the depressed feelings that had been so evident in recent days. As he was driving home, his mind turned to another line of thought. He remembered what Helen had said that morning just before he'd left for work. "I've had some headaches and nausea lately," she'd said. *Nausea . . . could that mean what I think it means?* he wondered. That morning he'd been thinking only of himself and dreading his return to work and had hardly heard what she'd said. Suddenly he became very concerned about the matter and drove quickly home.

Bob pulled into the driveway and came to a screeching stop. Before the car could come to a complete stop, he had the door open and was stepping out. Helen met him at the door. Her face was beaming; obviously her recent discomfort was not a result of any serious problem. Bob stepped inside the door and hung his jacket in the closet then removed his footwear. Only rarely had he seen his wife behave this way. Normally she was well able to control her emotions, but this time was different. She remained close to him, smiling and talking constantly, obviously trying to mask the jubilation she was experiencing. A weight had been lifted at the doctor's office; she had been much concerned that her condition may have been serious. Although it was serious, very much so, it would not be fatal, and she wanted to share the verdict with her husband. Bob put his arms around her, and she looked up into his eyes. For the first time, he detected a glint of mischief about them. As he nodded his head to kiss her, she continued to bubble with enthusiasm. It was quite obvious to Bob that she was having difficulty containing herself, but why? He had no idea as to the reason for her strange action. Nothing in his past had prepared Bob for the news he was about to receive. "What did the doctor have to say today, hon?" he said.

There! she thought. *There's no need to contain it any longer.* "He said that you and I are going to be parents," she said.

"WHAT?"

She began to speak again; this time Bob was paying strict attention to every word she said. "The doctor said that come late January or early February, you and I will have another mouth to feed. Isn't that great?"

Yes, it is great, Bob thought, but he didn't answer her; he couldn't. He cried. Tears of joy ran down his cheeks and off his chin. He tried to talk and couldn't; he could only blubber his heartfelt approval. He felt foolish because of his inability to mouth the words he wanted to say, so he stopped trying to say anything. He stood for some time, holding Helen and trying to pull himself together.

Bob was a big man, rough and tough; he stood and faced life, took all it could throw at him, and never gave an inch. In the years to follow, Helen would look back on many things many times. She would remember her husband for all the strengths he possessed. Her fondest memory of Bob, however, would always be the recollection of him standing with her in his arms, sobbing, trying desperately to control the sheer joy that this news had produced within him. He had a heart that his chest could scarcely contain, a love that radiated from within, and now he'd have one more loved one to share it with.

Helen began teaching that year with the understanding that she'd work only until the Christmas break. After the holidays, she'd remain at home and prepare for the arrival of the youngster. As the days went slowly by, she found herself wrapped up in a quest for baby clothes. Bob had to finally holler "Whoa" when she gathered enough sleepers, diapers, and booties for five babies. He too, however, lived with a continuing anticipation as the days turned into weeks, the weeks into months, and finally Christmas was only two weeks away.

Young William Robert Walker came into the world on a cold day in late January. Even as a newborn, he made quite an impression. The nurse, when measuring the boy, found that the regular tape was two inches too short. She smiled and shook her head, then sent for a longer one. Billy was nine pounds eleven ounces, big and healthy. The doctor smacked him on the bottom, and the first announcement was made of young Bill's arrival. His cry echoed through the delivery room, an assurance that all was well with the child.

Bob could not have possibly been more pleased as he made foolish faces and carried on behind the pane of glass that separated the babies from the public. He talked on and on about the child. Over and over he'd repeat the same phrases, expounding on the obvious merits of his new son. Other young fathers arrived to view their newborns; they came and went, but Bob remained at the window for hours. According to him, there had never been a more handsome, perfectly formed, alert child born than young Bill.

While Helen was in the hospital, Bob missed her greatly. He spent many of the lonely hours thinking of the coming years and how he'd like to see young Bill grow up. It was then that he decided to seriously plan a departure from the city. Having no idea when or exactly how the exodus would come about, Bob nevertheless made up his mind, and there certainly would be a farewell to urban dwelling. Young Billy was not going to grow up breathing the smoke and the smog that his father had always known. Insomuch as circumstances depended on Bob, he and his family would breathe clean air and eat natural foods whenever possible.

Once again Bob threw himself into his work but this time with a new purpose in mind. He was determined to leave the concrete jungle behind, and Helen was just as determined to help in every way she could. With the new goal they'd set for themselves came a new zest for living. Within a few weeks, Helen returned to work, and another wage was added to help them build up their escape fund.

Bob's parents were retired; they felt that the sun shone through young William's eyes, so there were certainly no babysitting problems. Helen felt good about leaving the child in the care of family members; she knew that Billy would be well looked after. His grandparents were thankful for being in a position from which they could truly help out, and all things considered, the situation could not have worked out better.

With both Bob and Helen working again and cutting corners, the bank account began to grow. Bob began to see that there was a light shining at the end of the tunnel. The hope he'd known began to grow, and his doubts slowly faded as his dream came nearer to reality. Within a few years, an opportunity arose for Bob, the chance that he once had dreamed of. He was offered a building contract, the only stipulation being that he must personally take charge. It would be necessary that he spend long hours away from home, and many of his weekends would be taken up as well. Bob seriously considered the opportunity for a time. Accepting the position would bring their moving date much closer, quicker. With the added responsibility, he'd receive more than enough to buy the things for his wife and child that he wanted to—presents that up until then seemed a frivolous waste of money. He thought long about accepting, and then he rejected the whole idea.

Sometime in the past, Bob had read somewhere that children need a father's presence much more than they need his presents. Believing this strongly, Bob applied the wisdom of the statement to his relationship with his wife as well and happily turned down the possible venture that came masquerading as an opportunity. They would just have to take their time and be patient. *Success comes to those who wait*, he thought.

CHAPTER 16

I F BY RECEIVING material success, a man undermines and weakens his personal strengths, then it would seem that there is little success and much foolishness. Putting the opportunity for promotion behind him, Bob went on with his job as if the offer had not been made. There were those who found it hard to believe that he had taken the position he had. They could see only the immediate situation, however, and not the long term. There are those who cannot understand that the material gain of this world, at best, is a poor imitation for the real important things. Bob's first concern was the welfare of his family. His health and peace of mind depended directly upon their welfare. He did not try to rationalize his decision to those he worked with. Whether they agreed or disagreed with him made very little difference. The war had taught him a valuable lesson—consider the alternatives, take the initiative, make a decision, then whether wrong or right, live with that decision. The decision had been made, and he felt that because of it, he and his family would benefit. Only time would tell whether or not the conclusion Bob had reached would turn out for the better. He felt that the good of his family was ultimately the most important aspect behind the stand he took.

Bob loved being home with his wife and child, and he felt anything that enabled him to do that could not be wrong. There came a certain peace to him when he put the happiness of his family on a higher plane than the desire for material gain.

He had crossed one more hurdle that had been standing between himself and their plan to live on the lake. Had the job opportunity not been offered, he'd never have known whether or not he was good enough to succeed in a more responsible position. The fact that he definitely was, had now been established, and he was content in the knowledge that he could certainly have advanced. He had the respect of his peers, and really, isn't that what it's all about? Bob was not one to look back; the decision had been made. He remained satisfied with himself for making it, but it helped to know that he had a choice.

On the day that Billy turned five, his parents and grandparents made a big event out of it. Helen made preparations for a party, young Bill's first. There were noisemakers and party hats, ice cream, cake, and jelly beans. The grownups beamed with delight as Billy and his little friends gobbled up the goodies and created enough noise to bring the house down. Bob's parents were most thankful that they were young enough to be able to really enjoy their grandchild. They commented that they should certainly live to enjoy the others that they were sure Bob and Helen would have. Bob's dad pampered little Billy almost to the point of spoiling him. His mother would hold him in her arms and speak as though he was the only child in the world, and Bob supposed for her, he was. That evening after supper, Billy's grandparents went to their own home. Again they made a fuss over the rambunctious young fellow. The way they carried on, one would almost think that they'd never see him again.

They didn't! Four days later, Bob's mom was killed in a car accident, and his dad was left clinging to life by a thread. Bob and Helen arrived at the hospital just as the orderlies were wheeling Bob's father into surgery. They could tell from a distance that he was bruised and badly shaken up. As he was quickly moved along the corridor, Bob got a fleeting look at a man he barely recognized. His father was in a coma, his body broken and bleeding from the high-speed impact. The two had been on their way home from the theater when it happened. A bank had been robbed, and the police were in a high-speed pursuit of the getaway car. His parents were halfway through an intersection when the cars collided. The escaping vehicle hit his father's car broadside in the center of the passenger's door. Bob's mother didn't have a chance.

CHAPTER 17

H OURS LATER, BOB'S dad was wheeled into intensive care. It was days before he regained consciousness. Weeks passed before there was any meaningful conversation between them. Bob did a lot of thinking during those weeks. His relationship with his dad had always been one of mutual respect. Very little real, heartfelt emotion, though, had been evident between them throughout the years. Although they'd always been devoted to one another and there was certainly a deep feeling of caring, somehow they never got around to actually saying it. Bob wished that he had told his dad more about the way he felt. When the two began to converse once more, Bob did tell his father that he loved him and how scared he'd been of losing him.

Will, Bob's dad, was not a big man; Bob got his size from his mother's side. Will was somewhat less than six feet tall; his character, though, made him stand as a giant among men. He had a sentimentality that would allow him to silently weep when he was deeply moved. The words that Bob spoke to him that day produced just such a response. Bob tried desperately to keep the conversation from turning to his mother, but his dad would not have it. *If Bob was determined to evade the subject,* he thought, *then I'll raise it,* and raise it he did.

Will was aware that his wife had been killed in the accident, and he had accepted it. He knew too that if he were ever to leave the hospital and attempt to go on without her, he'd need help. Realistically, he tried to get Bob to understand that a solution could not be found if he continued to deny that there was a problem. Will was further down the road toward acceptance than Bob was in regard to the untimely death of his wife and Bob's mother, Sharon.

"Can you remember, Bob, as a little boy, your mother used to say, 'A person's dying is more an affair for the survivors than for the deceased?' She tried in her own way to prepare you for an event that comes to all of us. People who fear death die a little each time they think of it. She would say,

'Surely you realize that your mother did not fear death.' Rather, she spoke of dying as being promoted. A wise man once said, 'He is no fool who gives up what he cannot keep to gain what he cannot lose.' Shortly thereafter, he was murdered by the very people he'd gone to minister to. That man gave up the temporary and gained the eternal. Your mother is much better off where she is, Bob, make no mistake about that. If we remember that fact, we'll be able to better accept her going. When you were a child, she taught you to read the Bible and to believe in God. We can be certain that she wants nothing now. She has gone home!"

Bob's eyes filled with tears as the love and respect welled up within him. Love that had lain dormant for years now came rushing back to him. Like a torrential flood it came, filling his heart and soul. The effects that the spirit brought with him included things long forgotten. Things that he really had never understood became real to him. His father had touched on a subject that had seemingly died somewhere in North Africa, amid exploding mortar shells, hand grenades, and the unceasing screams of young soldiers. Boys had begun the campaign champing at the bit, so to speak, unable to wait for combat. When it came, these same boys were left badly wounded, dying, or worse, lying in pools of their own blood, halfway around the world from home. Bob had been there; he'd seen it and was unable to believe the depths to which man was willing to go just to gain a few more feet of ground. He shuddered as the pictures flashed before his mind. Somewhere during those first few days of combat, Bob's faith had been shaken and had not recovered until now. He felt good!

It was hard to say who felt better about what had just happened; was it Bob or was it his father? In any case, Will had been watching and waiting for a long time, wondering what it was that had produced such a change in his son. Once Bob's emotional dam had burst, it became much easier for him to talk about the part of his life that he had always been so secretive about. He found that the more he opened up about the war and discussed the atrocities of it, the better he felt. His father had been able to read between the lines and sensed that the tension of the situation was beginning to have profound effects on his son's mind. This release of emotions was the safety valve that loosened the tension.

That evening Bob sat in the living room reading a book when a thought occurred to him. *Here is this man, my father, who is cut and bruised, scarred, and trussed up in casts to support healing bones. He'd been battered, operated upon, and needed assistance to sit up in bed. On top of all this, he lost his wife of forty-seven years to a speeding fugitive from justice, and he's witnessing to me, making me feel better when he has got to be hurting terribly himself.*

That's confident living. Today I have been truly fortunate, Bob thought. He learned more about his dad in that one day than he had during the balance of his lifetime.

Bob worried about his father in the weeks that followed. His body was slow to mend, and he became increasingly discouraged. He seemed to have lost the will to recover on that early day in March when Bob went to visit. Will was out of the hospital then but still could not get around by himself. He had a full-time nurse who lived in and tended to his needs. It was Bob's turn to do the cheering up, and he felt woefully inadequate for the task.

CHAPTER 18

I FORGOT WHO SAID that life can be like an onion—you peel it off one layer at a time, and sometimes it makes you weep. So it was that morning when Bob walked across the lawn and stood in front of the big house where he had grown up. Along the way he stopped to reminisce a bit and allowed his mind to drift back through the years. First, he remembered the day that his draft notice arrived. He'd stood out there that day too. With stars in his eyes, he put on a mock display of an infantry man marching in full battle display. Then, he thought there was honor in war. Where was honor? When the horror of war came with a vengeance, young men on both sides were left facedown in the mud, some dead instantly, others left to drown in the bloody water. Others watched in disbelief, stripped even of their vain pride, which had so cunningly led them to the enlistment office.

Taking a few more steps, Bob looked up, and his eyes focused on the metal hoop that still hung on the garage. Many an hour was spent with his father here playing one-on-one with the basketball. The hoop was rusty, and the mesh basket had rotted and fallen off, but the memories were fresh. As if it had happened yesterday, Bob could see his dad, young and agile with a head full of blond hair. His father was taking a breather, bent over, hands on his knees, catching his second wind. But he really wasn't, was he? No, he was upstairs, an old man now, burned out, but the memories were so real.

Then Bob recalled an unlikely event from his past. It took him all the way back to his first day of school. Ricky Baker was a neighbor of theirs, and both being the same age, needless to say they started school together. Both these kids were testy little fellows with the full intention of being the dominant kid on the block. A fight ensued, and young Bob lost. He came home with a black eye; he was bruised, and the chip he was carrying on his shoulder was far too big for any child to bear. What he wanted to do to Ricky Baker could have filled a book. But when he talked it over with his dad, thinking that he might get some pointers as to how he should go about it, he did get some pointers all right, but they were not in regard to furthering his fighting career. What he did say didn't make much sense to Bob; after all, Ricky had started it.

Will said to Bob, "I wonder what would have happened today if you'd have let Ricky have his way. Chances are, there'd have been no fighting, no harsh words, not even a disagreement. You know, most things that men disagree about are really not important over the long term. We must learn to give a little. If and when we do, people tend to accept us quicker." The youngster didn't really understand all that his dad had said, but he decided to apply that which had made some sense. Within days he found that the "giving in" approach was beginning to work. Not only did the new attitude make Bob feel better, but Ricky began to apply it as well. Bob never came home with a black eye again, and the two boys remained friends.

After Ricky's family moved, Bob missed his friend and found himself back in his dad's study for more advice. "Friends will come and go as will those you love. Sometimes it seems as though we are constantly saying good-bye to the people we care for, but we must learn to accept it. When I was a boy, I recall hearing a proverb that made a lot of sense to me. I have carried it with me since then. If we are to make a friend and maintain that friendship, we must show ourselves to be a friend. Bob, if you can apply this truth, you'll have no shortage of people who truly care for you."

Bob's dad had always been available to him to share the wisdom he'd acquired through the years. He was there too when Bob, first learning to ride his bike, fell down and skinned his knee. Will was also there when he was cut from the junior high basketball team. "Too short," the coach said after the young man had worked so hard and practiced for hours, day after day. Bob had stood in the entry, tears rolling down his cheeks. His father walked up to him, took Bob's head between his hands, and placed it on his chest. Will didn't have anything to say, so he quietly waited for the hurt to pass. *Yes, Dad was always there*, Bob thought. He almost always knew what to say, and even when he did not, somehow Bob felt that his dad had always shared his pain. He cared deeply, and sometimes, even in silence, he could communicate in a way that words will never know. He was there, he cared, and that had made all the difference.

Now it was Bob's turn to show that he cared. With the death of his mother still fresh in his mind, he had difficulty finding the proper words. He had come not knowing who would comfort who but nevertheless needing the closeness of family during this time of grief.

Bob was standing at the foot of the stairs when the nurse approached him. "I believe your father is sleeping," she said. "Go on up and sit with him if you like." Bob climbed the stairs as he'd done so many times in the past. He could almost hear his mother's voice echo through the building, threatening him with bodily harm if he didn't quit running up and down those stairs. He stopped at the top of the staircase, sat down with head in hands, and the tears flowed freely once more.

Why is it that we never truly appreciate our loved ones until they are gone? Only then do we think of things we should have done and words we should have said but didn't, he thought.

Continuing down the hall to his father's room, Bob wiped his eyes dry with his hanky in an effort to hide the hurt he was feeling. Reaching the door, he turned and went in. His father was sleeping quietly; lying beside him on the bed was a picture of Bob's mother. Will had been reminiscing before he fell asleep. His mind had taken him back in time to a day shortly before they'd been married. Sharon was all dressed up in her Sunday best. She stood in the garden in her gingham dress and lace stockings, ringlets of hair covering her shoulders and highlighted by bright red bows. There could never be another as fair as his garden rose named Sharon. Holding the picture of his loved one firmly in his mind, Will had slipped into a deep sleep.

Bob turned to leave the room, not wanting to wake his dad and spoil his dreams of better days. He had taken only a few steps when his father awoke. "Leaving so soon?" he said. "Come, crank this bed up, and we'll talk."

Will couldn't help but notice his son's bloodshot eyes, and the puffiness too made it clear that Bob had been grieving. "I'm not the only one who's finding this situation hard to bear up to, am I, son?" Bob never said anything; he just nodded his head in agreement. "Sitting here day after day doesn't make it any easier either. If I could just get up and do things, keep myself busy, I'm sure coping would be much easier. Bob, I'm not ever going to walk again, I know that. The doctor showed me the x-rays of my legs. The bones are smashed. Now they may heal to a degree, I hope they do," he said. "I may even be able to get around the house eventually. At best though, I'll never again be able to fend for myself. My life from now on will depend on the help and patience of others. There will be things that I can do, however, and writing poetry is one of them. I could never seem to find the time before, even though I've always loved forming verses that rhyme. If only my arm heals well enough to enable me to hold a pen.

"That reminds me, do you remember the game we used to play when you were a child? I'd form a short line of verse, and then you'd try to think of a second line. I used to love those times we had together." Tears clouded his eyes as he thought back once again. "I used to love to run through the fields of standing grain and to climb up high in the hills, look into the valley, and watch over all the beauty that has gone into its creation. The long walks are over for me now. I won't climb another hill to sit on a stump and feel the closeness of God. Don't let these tears fool you, son, for though there certainly is remorse in this old heart, there is also contentment. The Lord has allowed this affliction to come into my life, but though he has sent sorrow, he has also sent grace sufficient to sustain me. I don't know why he has allowed this thing. Perhaps it will become clear in time.

"I hoped you'd find time to visit today," he said. "I have a proposition for you to consider. I am alone now, alone, and in need of care. I've never considered myself to be a demanding person, but there are things that I will never be able to do for myself. This house is plenty big enough for all of us, so I want you to talk to Helen about moving in with me. Would you do that for me? Being close to the two of you and having my grandson here will make all the difference. Bob, talk to Helen, take your time in making a decision."

Bob promised his father that he'd seriously consider the offer, and then he left his side. Somewhere on the way home, he realized that his dad had done it again. Bob had gone into Will's bedroom wondering how he was going to handle the situation. What could he say to comfort the man he loved most in the world? Where would he begin, and could he keep from breaking down? Bob had not even realized it at the time, but from the moment his father had awakened, he had carried the conversation. "Can you beat that?" he said to himself. "Some men are just better listeners than talkers, I suppose." Bob was witnessing a facet of his father's character that he had no way of appreciating until now. Maybe even his dad didn't realize how deeply his faith was imbedded. From the attitude that his dad had taken toward the accident, the death of his wife, and the crippling of his own body, it was obvious that he was trusting all to the will of God.

Bob talked to Helen about his father's proposal, and she could see merit in the plan. There were, of course, difficulties that would have to be worked out. For the most part, however, she approved of the idea.

She immediately began to make some phone calls in an attempt to find a babysitter. Hopefully, they could find someone who'd come in from eight in the morning until four in the afternoon, someone who'd agree to prepare lunch for Will and watch him as well as young Billy until Helen arrived home from school. After some time, Helen found just such a person. She'd interviewed a number of applicants and screened them all, rejecting each one until it came time to talk to Karen. Karen was a woman in her fifties, a widow who'd lost her husband in a hunting accident. The accident had happened just a few months prior to the interview, and Karen was still shocked by her loss and adjusting to it. She was a very pleasant individual who lived within walking distance, a fact that was beneficial to both parties.

Bob and Helen listed their home, and shortly after the sign went up on the front lawn, it sold. It was a comfortable house in a good location, and they had asked a fair market price for it, which was the main reason for the quick sale. Helen was not overjoyed; she had mixed feelings about the situation. Many memories flooded her mind as she took one last stroll through the house and walked out onto the patio, which overlooked the backyard. She was near the point of breaking down when Bob carried the last piece of furniture out of the house. "Let's get out of here before this gets messy," she said. "The very idea, getting all choked up over an empty house." But it was not the house she'd miss as much as the memories.

CHAPTER 19

M UCH OF THEIR furniture was stored in Will's garage; they didn't need it. Little by little they sold it and put the money in what they'd come to call their wilderness fund. With the scale of the house and the profit it brought, they now had more than they'd need to make the move. Living with Bob's father would cut expenses even more, and the fund would continue to grow.

Weeks turned into months, and as the seasons changed, Will sat by his bedroom window and looked out on the activity of the city. Even in the relatively quiet residential area where they lived, there was evidence of the fast-paced, always-in-a-hurry way of life. It seemed to him that some people never had enough time to enjoy themselves. They'd rush off to work early in the morning, return late in the evening with hardly enough time to eat supper before bedtime. The following day they'd follow exactly the same schedule. Day in and day out they'd repeat the ritual; how could they continue with no leisure time on their schedule? He couldn't understand it; it was never the intention for man to work all the time.

There was a soreness that daily grew more intense in Will's right hip. He pushed and poked at the area in an effort to find its exact location. Will hoped that the medication he was taking would alleviate the soreness, but a week went by, and the inflamed area continued to get worse. The tender area gradually became larger, and when he could no longer swing himself from the bed to his wheelchair, he was forced to disclose the facts to Bob.

Bob, of course, phoned the doctor immediately, and that night Will slept in a hospital bed. Many tests were run to establish the cause of the soreness as Will's condition continued to get worse. As the infected area grew, so too did its effect on Bob's father. The poisons given off began to travel through his body, and Will became a very sick man. As the days dragged on, there remained no change in his condition; by and large, the tests produced nothing concrete as to what the cause was. Will became so weak he needed help to raise his head for a drink of water. His condition was such that even the tone of his skin had changed. The poisons began to affect the normal functions of some of Will's other organs. At times, Will had no control of them; it seemed almost as though he'd become a baby once again. When the doctor entered the room and declared that they had discovered the source of his problem, Will didn't even have enough energy to smile, though he certainly was encouraged by the words.

Because of the fact that Will's bones had been so slow to heal, he had become accustomed to living with pain; therefore, he had been slow to detect the effects of the new infection. He'd been living with so much hurt for so long that a little more or less had not registered. Like all infections, if left unchecked, they begin to spread. This infection began to develop and acquired a snowball-like effect. The longer it was allowed to roll along undetected, the bigger it became. The larger it got, the stronger the poisons became and the harder they were to control. The doctor was holding the results of Will's most recent blood tests; however, they showed a marked improvement over the previous ones. The infection was beginning to give way to the bombardment of antibiotics, and it appeared as though Will was on his way to recovery. Although not quite out of the woods, he was pointed in the right direction. Bob and Helen were feeling quite good about the improvement in Will's condition. They looked forward to his return home, which was to be within a few short days. He had been taken off intravenous fluids and was once again eating solids. His color had improved, and he was sleeping much better. Recovery was slow; he had sunk to such a state that it took days before improvement was evident. A confidence was creeping back into Will's heart. He had been very much demoralized throughout the affair, but slowly his smile was returning; he even managed to joke with the nurses. The medication was effecting increasing improvement, and it seemed certain that Will's condition would continue to improve.

The reports Bob had been receiving from their family doctor in regard to his dad's condition were encouraging, to say the least. He and Helen were certain that his dad would be home within a few days. They had no way of knowing that the details of those reports would prove to be the calm before a storm. Because the news had been so favorable for days, Bob and his wife were not prepared for the telephone call they received early one Saturday morning. It was late September when the phone rang and then rang again. Waking from a deep sleep, Bob wiped the sleep from his eyes and then reached for the phone. He recognized the voice of the doctor even though he was still feeling the effects of what had been a very good night's rest. Wondering why the doctor would phone so early, he listened as the horror story was unfolded to him. "Your father," the doctor said, "has come through a very difficult night. In his weakened condition, he has contracted pneumonia. One lung has collapsed, and the other is about to, I'm afraid. He appears to have used up most of the reserve he'd regained since his bout with the infection. His condition was progressing so well, this has taken us totally by surprise. I knew you'd want to come down, Bob. It doesn't look good!"

Surprise showed on Bob's face; he could not believe how sudden this was. He remembered thanking the doctor for making the phone call, and after hanging up, Bob just sat there holding on to the receiver, as if paralyzed by the information he'd just received. Helen stirred and asked, "What was that all about?" She took hold of the phone and put it to her ear; it was dead. Hanging up the receiver, her gaze fell on Bob as she asked, "Bad news?"

"Dad's condition has deteriorated to the point where the doctor thinks we should come and see him. He's got pneumonia. It doesn't look good!" he said. "I can't believe it. Only yesterday Dad was doing so well."

When they arrived at the hospital, Will's body was once again inserted with an intravenous tube. He wore an oxygen mask, and a machine recorded each heartbeat. He looked ghastly as he lay there not knowing or caring that his children had come. There was very little sense in their remaining, except that it made them feel better. Will drifted in and out of consciousness, opening his eyes from time to time but not really understanding what was going on around him. The doctor had been right, and Bob's worst fears were realized late that same afternoon. Wills' second lung collapsed, and in the weakened condition that had been caused previously by the infection, he simply did not have the strength to fight any longer. Bob was in the hospital waiting room when the doctor approached him with the bad news. "Your father has died, Bob. His condition just demanded more than he had left to give."

Bob stood up and took the doctor's hand, thanking him. With tears in his eyes, he said, "There'll be no more pain and suffering for him now. He's gone home to be with Mom. He'll be happy there." The doctor smiled to show his approval, then walked away to continue his work.

Helen had gone home early to prepare supper, so Bob took a taxi and arrived just as she was about to phone the hospital. He came into the house, head hung low, choking back the tears and making a poor attempt at controlling his emotions. Helen did not need to ask about his father. She could tell from Bob's actions that his dad had passed away. She walked over to her husband and put her arms around his neck. They hugged each other as the tears flowed freely. Just as they'd shared everything else in their recent lives, they now shared their grief. "There's no one left but us now. Just us, Bob. No one in this whole world for Bill but you and me."

Bob looked at his wife and said, "You know, I don't remember a time when Dad didn't talk of nature. He always said that he was going to leave the city. Dad wanted to leave so bad that tears would fill his eyes when he spoke about it. He wanted a little white country home, a barn, and a workshop. He spoke too of the picture that he'd formed in his mind over the years. The barn had to be situated in exactly the right spot, as did all the other buildings. He'd draw pictures for Mom and I, rough blueprints of the layout. 'Someday,' he'd say, 'We're going to leave this jungle of steel and concrete and get back to the land where we should be.' He wanted a vegetable garden and some strawberry plants, a few berry bushes, and an apple tree. He'd never managed to put aside enough money to break free though, so he learned to be content with what he and Mother had here. I wonder if he has his apple tree now."

CHAPTER 20

WITHIN A FEW weeks, life began to return to normal for Bob and Helen although it didn't seem like home with Dad gone. He had become an important part of a closely knit family. Even Billy, as young as he was, realized that something was missing, someone was gone. Billy was miserable for days; Will had spent a good deal of time with the boy, and he'd come to rely on it. Time has a way of healing all wounds though, especially with the young. Soon the youngster was channeling his affections in other directions, and his young mind became attached to another individual. Karen was the lady who'd answered the ad that Helen had placed. She'd been tending Will and babysitting Billy for some time. Only after Will's death, however, did she and the boy become close friends.

Billy was like his grandfather in many ways; he even looked much like Will. Will, of course, was a small man, but Billy appeared to have inherited his father's size. Temperament and character traits that were evident in the young man truly spoke of his grandfather, and Bob was glad for that. He'd loved his father very much. He looked forward to a day when he would be able to spend more time with his boy. Bob's father had a dream that was never fulfilled; now the dream had become Bob's. Bob's plan was different though; it involved more than a hobby farm in the country. He continued to long for a home in the wilderness where Bill could grow and develop, breathe fresh air, and live off the land, where Bob could grow with his son and enjoy watching him as he matured. Only time spent together can produce a friendship between two individuals, and Bob wanted to be his son's friend. He wanted to teach Billy the things he'd learned about the wild, and he knew that there were many things they could learn together. First, though, a break had to be made with civilization. It would not be easy to make that break; all the security they knew in the world was closely tied to city life. Helen had said she was in favor of the move. Bob was certain that he wanted to go, but there still remained one family member who had to be considered: Billy. Was pulling up stakes here and embarking on a new way of life in his best interest? Would it be possible to provide him with a suitable education by correspondence? Would he be a child who'd excel in and enjoy the wilderness? Would it restrict him later in life when dealing with people who would not know his wilderness ways? There were so many questions for Bob to consider and so few answers.

When Bob's mother had been killed and his father disabled, he and Helen had decided to move to Will's home. They had made a commitment to Bob's father, and even though they hadn't considered it at the time, that action had extended their stay in the city. When difficulties come to a family member, all else becomes of secondary importance. Will was gone now; he no longer required their assistance. Shortly after his passing, the healing process began, and Bob was able to get on with his life. As the weeks turned into months, he and Helen began to speak once again about the valley of the Big Salmon River and how they'd enjoyed their holiday there.

Spring came once again, and as the snow melted and the water ran off the roof, into the eaves trough, and down the spout to the cement driveway. Bob sat by the window watching the city maintenance crew sweep the salt and sand from the sides of the street. It had been a long winter with a heavy snowfall; the city's expense had been high. Dust and dirt, soot and sand had accumulated on the snow during the long months. With the snow melting, it all came together to produce a filthy-looking black blanket that covered the boulevards. It was not a pretty sight and only added more fuel to the desire that continued to burn within him. For a long time, his mind had been made up; he wanted to go, and he would. It was never a question of whether he wanted to leave, but rather of when. He'd struggled with a number of questions, found few answers; some could not be answered by any means except through the passage of time.

The day came when the final papers arrived from Will's lawyer; they were to be signed and returned. Within a few days, Bob received legal information concerning his father's will; being an only child, he had inherited all of his father's possessions.

Bob held Helen once again and said, "It had to come to this, I suppose. It's sad that this is all I have left of Dad. How can this compare with what we've lost?"

Helen stated, "You know it can't, Bob, but if he were watching now, it may be that he'd say, 'Now you can follow your dream.'"

As Bob was standing there, he lowered his head and said, "We're going to follow the dream, Helen, starting right now." He phoned the real estate office and listed their home for sale. Helen had left her roots behind them when they'd sold her father's home; now it was Bob's turn.

CHAPTER 21

B OB QUIT HIS job and concentrated on selling their household effects. There would be no roads where they were going, no moving vans, and no possibility of transporting heavy furniture across the lake. Only the most basic of furniture would be needed, and they'd purchase that up north. Everything was for sale, and Bob was now available to speak to prospective buyers. He could take the necessary time to establish a fair price for the items. The task was time-consuming; they had not yet sold many of the items that had been put into storage when they moved from Helen's home. Bob began an advertising campaign, which consisted of running newspaper ads and enlisting the help of the real estate people. Because Bob had prepared well for the sale of the secondhand furniture, the results were encouraging. By establishing fair prices, he had appealed to many who became serious shoppers. Sales went so well that they were soon forced to eat their meals on the kitchen counters because even the table and chairs were sold. Fridges, the deep freezer, chesterfield suites, beds, linen, and then Helen's rolltop desk, even the old china cabinet was sold. They had to buy a hot plate to heat their food, and they began to live out of a can. Once a day they were forced to go out for a meal. They never dreamed they'd have the success they did. Then the house sold, and they'd passed the point of no return. There were no doubts in Bob's mind about the decision they'd made, but Helen was not quite as sure as he was. She remained concerned about the fact that there were no roads in the area, no quick way to receive help if it were needed. Bob assured her that any needed help would only be a few hours away. He planned to purchase a radiophone; it would take only seconds to reach Whitehorse and have an airplane sent to the lake with any needed help. Helen assured herself that her misgivings were only last-minute jitters. She'd felt the same way on the night before their wedding, and she'd always be thankful for going along with it. *This would be so different*, she thought. *Once we're there, I'll be all right.*

The day arrived when the house they'd come to treasure became the property of new owners. The money was placed into their bank account; Bob had received a check for the agreed price. Nothing remained in the entire city to hold them back or delay their departure any longer. They packed their clothing into four suitcases, loaded them into the trunk, started the car, and backed it out of the driveway. Those suitcases and the canoe that rode on top of the car were all that remained of all that they'd possessed in the city. Undoubtedly, this was a decision of paramount proportions, unlike any they'd ever made before or ever would again. Helen looked back over her shoulder as the car rounded the corner. Bob never took a backward glance; his eyes were focused on the road ahead, and that was where they remained. He had finally made the break he'd been planning for years. He would not allow himself to ponder the things that were; he smiled and contemplated the things that were to come.

As they entered the freeway, Bob stepped on the gas pedal. He seemed to be in a hurry to get started, but Helen would have none of it. "It would be nice to get there in a hurry, Bob, but if you keep this up, we may not get there at all." Looking down at the speedometer, he quickly realized that she was right and immediately adjusted the speed. Continuing at a reduced speed, Bob began to sing some familiar songs, and it was not very long until Helen joined in. Soon even Billy was trying hard to follow the tune, and as the hours went by, Helen began to lose the inhibitions she'd recently acquired. When a person becomes comfortable in their lifestyle, they can conform so closely to it that change becomes almost impossible. Helen had become so comfortable that she'd almost forgotten the dream she'd shared with her husband. Within the few days that followed, her mood continued to improve, and when they reached Whitehorse, she became quite involved with Bob's plans once again.

Bob's first stop was the bank; he transferred his account to Whitehorse where he'd be doing business. He then went to the government office and signed a lease on the lakeshore property where the little cabin nestled in the trees. That being completed, he contacted a local bush pilot whom he employed to fly them to the lake. Bob had to know how much weight the man's plane could carry. There would be many supplies to transport, heavy things like flour and potatoes. They had traveled light while camping on the lake, but this would be different; it was now to become their permanent home.

Fortunately, Bob found a pilot who flew over the lake on a regular basis. Harvey had contracts with a number of mining companies. These working mines were located near the lake and received supplies twice a week. Harvey would gladly stop by for coffee and pick up a grocery list one trip and then deliver the groceries the following trip if necessary. Bob was certain that they could function for more than a week at a time but was thankful for the sincere offer. Next, he went shopping for a freighter canoe. They'd need furniture, plywood, and lumber along with other items that were too bulky to carry in a plane. These items would have to be brought downriver, and a freighter would offer the means to accomplish the feat. Bob figured that an eighteen-footer would be ideal. To simplify the task of running the rapids, both upstream and down, he purchased a twenty-horsepower motor. "There," he said, "now we're set."

All the necessary preparations and purchases, large and small, took a few days to complete. Once they were completed, however, Bob loaded his pickup with lumber; the car had been traded in. He hooked the pickup to the boat and trailer and headed toward Quiet Lake. Helen remained in Whitehorse for a few days. She still had to register Billy and arrange for his correspondence schooling. She planned to come out within a few days by plane with Harvey. She'd probably arrive about the same time that Bob did. When Bob turned off the Alaska Highway and started up the South Canol Road, he giggled like a child. The dream was about to become reality, and thinking about it produced a childlike effect on him. He could not remember when he'd felt so good. Within two hours, he arrived at the lake and backed the trailer into the water. The freighter was unloaded, and then the supplies were transferred from the pickup to the canoe. The salesman had been right; he'd said that these boats will haul a lot of weight. Bob was surprised; the plywood, lumber, and furniture hardly made any difference. The craft sat high in the water, and Bob was sorry that he hadn't brought more building material. *Next trip, I'll know better*, he thought as he parked the truck and trailer.

Bob sat at the back of the freighter, feeling quite good about the whole situation. Making the necessary connections between the gas tank and outboard motor, he then squeezed the little ball that sent gasoline through the line to the motor. Placing the selector lever into neutral, he pulled on the starting cord. Once the engine had started, Bob reached over and checked the rope that secured the smaller canoe, which was in tow behind the big one. He then moved the selector handle to forward, and the canoe responded. As he increased the speed and began to feel the power at his fingertips, a feeling of satisfaction came over him that he had not felt before. He settled back into a comfortable position and smiled as the wind ruffled his hair. *This is the only way to go*, he thought. Bob was enjoying the trip immensely. The mouth of the river quickly drew closer, and Bob hadn't realized just how fast he'd been going until he looked back. The last time he'd been here, he and Helen had spent a day and a half crossing this expanse. As he approached the outlet to the river, he looked at his watch. Just shortly more than an hour ago, he had been making last-second adjustments to his cargo. Now here he was approaching the top of the rapids. He decided to go ashore and check the situation over before starting down the white water. As it turned out, he was glad he did, because a tree had fallen into the river. It would have blocked any passage Bob might have attempted. Hanging out over the swiftest portion of the rapids, it would have scuttled his canoe, destroyed the cargo, ruined the outboard motor, and quite possibly drowned Bob in the process. Returning to the canoe, Bob grabbed the axe, and soon he was hacking away at the tree that was still anchored in the ground by its root system. The constant washing of the water had undermined it until, being too heavy, it collapsed. Within minutes, Bob had chopped through the trunk, and the tree floated down the river.

The balance of the trip went without incident, and within hours Bob pulled his craft up to the beach that lay in front of the cabin, which from then on would be their home. He'd thought that Helen's arrival might precede his own, but having no difficulties along the way, he'd arrived much earlier than had been anticipated.

Helen arrived the following morning, and as Harvey circled to inspect the area, they saw Bob busily building a toolshed and storage building. When he heard the plane, he came running out on the beach, waving his arms and smiling. Helen smiled back; she knew that Bob had come home where he'd stay, and she was glad that it would be her home too. Bob was living his dream, something very few manage to do. Harvey set the plane down on the lake then came taxiing up to the beach. Helen and Billy climbed out and stood on the pontoon. Bob pulled the boat alongside to unload the groceries and take them to shore.

Life took on a new meaning for Bob and his family from that day forward. Their lives became increasingly intertwined as the years came and went. Young Bill grew strong and wise in the ways of the wilderness. As his body matured, so did his love for the lake, the valley, and the animals that also called it their home. Helen became increasingly contented as the necessary improvements were slowly accomplished. She was especially grateful for the change that had taken place in Bob. He loved the valley, and each new day was a brand-new experience for him.

The years brought trial and hardship, but they brought satisfaction too. It was a hard life that they wreaked out of the wild, but an honest one. When evening came, they were exhausted from a day's labor and never lay awake hoping for sleep to overtake their bodies. They were tired at night, and sleep came easily.

SID BELL

PART 2

CHAPTER 22

THE SUN ROSE over the treetops and danced on the water of Big Salmon Lake. A large Canada goose swam lazily with his family as they ate and prepared for their long flight south. A beaver swam with a purpose nearby, intent on finishing his house before the first snowfall.

At the point where the Big Salmon river flowed into the lake of the same name, a bull moose, in full mating display, broke the silence as he jumped over a windfall and came to rest on the beach. He stood there for a moment and sniffed the wind as a golden leaf fell from a tree and landed on the surface of the water. Satisfied that there was no danger, he lowered his head and drank from the clear, cold lake water.

At the far end of the lake, the water once again became a stream on its rendezvous with the Yukon River at Carmacks. On a sandy beach nearby, a single dog began to bark, then a second, followed by the whole team. Bob Walker rolled over, looked at the clock, and then swung a leg over the side of the bed. "Is the coffee on, Helen?" he said as another day began north of the sixtieth parallel.

Only then did Bob remember that the day before, he had caught some fish and hadn't gotten around to cleaning them. Normally he was meticulous about everything, but lately things hadn't been normal. As he fed the fish to the dogs, his mind drifted back to the events of the past few weeks.

The night had been black as death, but when morning came, the sun broke on a beautiful day. Helen was an early riser and was up before dawn. She was glad now for the daylight; she could see better to bake her bread. As the smell of fresh coffee filled the cabin, Bob thought that he was a very lucky man.

It had been two years since he felt this good about life. Two years. *Has it been that long?* he thought as his mind drifted back to their arrival on the lake.

Because Helen had been a schoolteacher before the decision was made to leave the concrete jungle and settle in the wilderness, young Bill took all his early schooling by correspondence then went to Whitehorse for high school. That boy had always been a source of pride for them, and they missed him very much. He was gone off and on for seven years before he finally came home to stay. He brought with him a degree in geology and planned to trap all winter then do soil and rock tests during the summer months.

It was Billy who'd bought the dog team and built the sleigh. They built a second cabin to serve as a soils lab for his equipment and rock samples.

Winter came early that year, and by the middle of September, the valley was blanketed with snow, but with Billy home again, the season just seemed to fly by.

They woke one morning to the sound of geese honking as they flew over the cabin. Bob looked at Helen and said, "Where did the winter go?" He went out with Bill to feed the dogs, and a warm breeze hit him in the face. He sat there on a block of wood and felt that God had truly smiled on this valley and everything in it.

Bill sat beside him and said, "I have never seen you this happy, Dad. Do you think you'll ever be sorry for leaving the city?" He didn't answer, he didn't have to, and Bill knew how his father felt about cities.

"Pancakes are ready" came a call from inside. He took Bill's arm, and they went into the cabin.

Time has a way of slipping away on people especially if they are happy about their lives. So it was that year! Spring slipped into summer, and soon the leaves began returning to color.

Bill spent most of his time searching the streams and combing the hills for signs of ore. Quite often he'd find deposits of silver lead but very little else. The Yukon was full of silver lead, most of it much more easily reached than what he'd found. However, he always carried his gold pan with him, and he was able to make wages for the work he did.

It was near the end of August when he decided to begin preparing the trapline for the season ahead. They worked together fixing any damage that had occurred to the cabins during the summer. They then concentrated on getting a winter supply of meat. By the time the meat drying and canning was complete, snow covered the ground. They were working on the dog harness when the first blast of cold air came out of the north. That first gust sent a chill up Bob's spine like none he had experienced before. He later remembered thinking at the time, *I wonder what is in store for us this winter.*

Little did he realize that that gust of wind was an omen of something that would shake the very foundation of all that he was.

From that day, the weather turned bad quickly. The mercury plunged to thirty below within a week, and by the middle of October, the temperature was well into the minus forties. God help them if Bill hadn't had the wisdom to read the signs of an early winter.

Conditions were terrible for them that first month, but their situation was nothing compared to that of the dogs. Winter, in all its fury, had hit so fast there was too little snowfall to cover the ground. The dogs were forced to exist in the impossible temperatures without any shelter. They put up a tent for them to huddle in, not really expecting it to help, and it didn't. The dogs, with the impossible conditions, became irritable, and some were downright mean. By the end of the month, they were in terrible shape, their resistance was gone, and they didn't even quarrel anymore. Then Jesse didn't come to be fed one morning; two days later Dan also died. That evening the sky clouded up, and a light breeze began to blow. The temperature rose twenty degrees, the snow began to fall, and the dogs sensed that the worst was over.

Helen stood looking through the window with a tear in her eye. She was watching the dogs that just lay there. She said, "Bob, what is it that makes people love a godforsaken land like this is?" He walked over and put his arm around her, kissed her on the cheek, and went to bed.

They awoke to a beautiful winter scene. Out on the lake, there were three moose, a cow, and two calves from the previous spring. The cow was watching the cabin intently while the calves played on what was probably their first experience with frozen water. They had certainly weathered the cold snap with no ill effects. Bob couldn't help but admire their beauty. Then he thought of the dogs and wondered how they were.

He went out to the porch, took some dried moose meat and frozen fish from the locker, and called to the dogs. "Laika, come on, girl," he called. "Come on, girl. There's a good dog." Nothing! He was just beginning to get concerned when the snow in front of him began to move. A few more quivers of snow then Laika stood up and came up to the porch. "I wonder how your partners are this morning, girl." He ran his hands up and down her large rib cage, gave her a good rubdown, and she began to wag her tail. He knew she was going to be all right. Thank goodness for that; he loved that dog best. Then Chico got up and came up to him, his tail in a tight curl over his back. Of all the dogs, he worried about Chico the least. He was the lead dog, and Bob knew his pride and determination would sustain him beyond anything the others could endure. He'd always felt that Chico must have some wolf blood in his veins. He was a beautiful animal, the picture of a perfect Siberian husky but much bigger. Chico could lope in harness for miles and still bring the others into line at the end of the day if they forgot that he was boss.

After Chico had eaten, and only then, did the other mounds of snow break. The rest of the team then ate their ration, and though some of them were slow to react, I knew the crisis was over.

In the following week, the weather wasn't quite so severe. Because they were warm and Bill began taking them for short runs with the sleigh, the dogs became content once again. Somehow they knew that the lazing around had almost come to an end. Each time Bill harnessed them up, their enthusiasm grew until the day he said, "They're ready. Now we can get on with life as it should be in the north."

Someone said a man is happiest when he works. So it was for Bill. From then on, he was obsessed with the trapline. Each morning began at six o'clock regardless of the weather conditions. Between running behind the sleigh all day and skinning his catch well into the evening, Bill had very limited conversation with his father.

Each day the dogs looked fresher and sleeker as they came across the lake in the late afternoon. Bill realized this, and it was then that he decided to extend his trips into the wilderness. They became longer until he was gone a week at a time and he was working the whole trapline.

And so it was for the next few weeks. One morning Bill woke early, put the coffee on, and was frying bacon and eggs when Bob awoke. "Dad, I'm going to take the day off, carve a few more stretchers, and just sit and talk." They had breakfast together, drank a pot of coffee, then went outside.

Chico saw them first; he was lying on a ledge that protruded out from the hill in front of the cabin. The ledge had become his, and heaven help any of the dogs who went near it. From there he could see everything that mattered to him in the world. From there he watched over the cabin, the sleigh, and the dogs. He could see far enough down the lake to know when an intruder would happen to stray into his domain.

Bill opened the door of the cache and fed the dogs. Chico had come down from the ledge and was standing at his feet. "What's wrong, fella? Can't you understand why you haven't been harnessed?" As Bill was giving Chico a good rubbing, Bob realized that there was a strong bond building between the two.

They went inside, and Bill motioned Bob over to the window. "Watch that dog of mine, Dad. He's quite an animal." Chico had gone straight back to his ledge and assumed his position as guard dog once again.

The following morning came, and the wind whistled around the cabin. Bill got the dogs ready and was off. The night before, he had said, "I'll be gone a week this time." Little did they know then that his leaving would lead to much more than a week's absence.

CHAPTER 23

ON THE SECOND day out, he stopped to check a trap. He removed a marten, then reset the trap and was about to go on his way. It was then that he noticed a number of ravens hovering in the distance. Ravens didn't do that unless they were feeding or about to feed. He guessed whatever it was that held their attention was less than a mile up Brown Creek. Curiosity demanded that he check this out, and he proceeded to do so. He knew that he could follow the creek up and come within feet of the ravens. When he arrived at the scene, a moose was lying down. There was blood on the snow all around her. The wolves were lying under a tree on top of the creek bed. They stood and bristled at Bill's arrival as three more appeared at the edge of the forest. Three shots from his rifle rang out, and the two largest wolves went down. The other three turned, entered the trees, and were gone. While Bill was dressing what remained of the moose, feeling that if nothing else it would make good dog meat, he heard it. A noise he had never heard before. It began as a low rumble and steadily grew until he could hear what sounded like trees snapping. Then he saw it coming down the mountain, gaining speed as it came. The moose, the wolves, everything was forgotten. The only important thing was to get out of there.

The sleigh had just been turned when it hit. Bill's screams and the yelps of the dogs were lost amid the roar of the avalanche. Dogs and man were rolled over and over; one second buried deep, the next carried to the surface. Bodies were crushed under the sheer weight of snow, rocks, and trees.

Then as quickly as it had started, the slide was over. Calm settled over the scene, and except for the odd rock and tree stump, one would never guess that it had ever been any other way.

So it was until a few minutes later when a raven flew down and began to pick away at the snow. Seconds later a tuft of hair broke the surface, and three more birds flew down to take their share of the moose meat.

Minutes went by, and then the ravens flew into the air as a dog began to whine directly beneath them. It was that whine, perhaps, that aroused Bill. He woke in what could have been a snowy grave two feet below the surface. As he slowly shook the cobwebs from his mind, he could have no idea of just how bad off he really was. Shortly, he composed himself enough to realize that he had to get to the surface. When he tried to move, he felt the pain.

Only then did he realize that he truly had a serious problem. This man had spent the major portion of his life in the bush. The years had taught him, among other things, that to panic would be fatal. He began to survey his situation as he knew it and to list the plus factors in his mind. Realizing that his leg had been broken, he tried to determine whether there were other injuries as well. Then a very important fact struck him: he had no trouble breathing; therefore, he had to be close to the surface. The next few minutes were spent positioning his arms in such a way as to reach over his head. When he did succeed in stretching his arms to their full length, he realized his hands were out of the snow.

Never had he experienced the pain that he endured for the next few hours. Pulling himself out of that snow was terribly painful, but it had to be done. The alternative was to lay there and freeze to death.

After what seemed like days but in fact was only a matter of minutes, Bill was on top of the snow mass. He rested awhile then looked at his leg. He felt he had been lucky; the slide had not killed him, and the leg was broken, but there was no compound fracture, and the cold snow had kept the swelling down. There were enough wood strips lying around from the broken sleigh to fashion a good splint for his leg.

Once his leg was bound up tight, he thought about the dogs. Only then did the pain subside enough to enable him to concern himself with anything but his own discomfort.

When he did think of the dogs, a feeling of guilt crossed his mind. He felt terrible about the fact that his own welfare had been the only thing that concerned him.

Where do I begin to look? he thought. Then he heard it again, low at first then more pronounced once the dog realized that someone was up there. Bill figured then that if the dog had lived this long, he was in no danger from shortage of oxygen. However, now that the dog knew Bill was there, he may damage himself through sheer excitement. In any case, the sooner he could be reached, the better.

In a few minutes, Bill had reached the dog and had cleared a space around the animal's head. If not for the harness, Chico could have gotten free himself, but he was anchored in place by the other dogs and the sleigh. Although the pain of his leg slowed him down, Bill worked steadily as was his nature; eventually he was able to cut the traces and free the dog.

Somehow Chico sensed that all was not right with Bill, and he watched over him closely as Bill collapsed due to complete exhaustion. When he woke, the sun had gone down, and he was without shelter. That night he huddled close to Chico for warmth. When morning came, the leg was inflamed and very sore, but Bill was determined to dig out the other dogs. It was late in the afternoon when he realized that there was no hope for the animals. Only then did he concentrate on erecting a shelter for himself. During his search for the dogs, he had uncovered two blankets and a pot. He then laid long sticks up against a large log that was lying down. In so doing, he had a makeshift lean-to, which was up against a sheer rock face. *Crude shelter*, he thought, but nevertheless an adequate windbreak. As a finishing touch, he made a floor inside the shelter with pine boughs in order to provide an airspace between himself and the frozen ground. In front of this, he built his fire, filled the pot with snow, and proceeded to make himself and Chico some boiled moose meat for supper.

Chico grew ever more restless through that night; he somehow knew that his master was in trouble. Morning came and Bill woke; his leg had swelled during the night, and there was a red line extending upward from his ankle to his knee. His pants had frozen to the ground during the night, and the pain wouldn't allow him to free himself.

He looked at Chico, who sat there looking like he could almost feel the pain that Bill was going through. "Come here, fella. We've spent a lot of good times together. Is this where it's going to end?" Then Bill got an idea. *I wonder if this animal is as smart as I think he is. Ever since we started working together, we've had a ritual. At the end of the day, when dusk started to fall, I would go up to Chico, rub his jowls, and say, "Home, boy, let's go home." Maybe, just maybe, it will work.*

He took Chico's head between his hands then rubbed his cheeks good and repeated, "Home, boy. Go on home." The dog looked in the direction of home then back at Bill. "Go on home, fella. Get Pa, go on, boy." He took one last look at Bill, whined, then without a backward glance, he was gone.

Bob was out on the porch the following morning getting an armful of wood for the fire when he saw it. Straight across the lake it came, never stopping or even slowing to sniff the wind. He thought then how odd it seemed that an animal would do that. Only once had Bob seen such a thing; the winter before, a moose had come across the lake that way. It came right up to the cabin and stayed within a hundred yards for two days. At the time though, they were sure that wolves had been the reason for that.

This was different; this animal appeared to be a wolf, much too big for a coyote. He went inside and grabbed the glasses to have a better look. Helen came out to witness this phenomenon, and she was beside him when he went limp. "Bob, what on earth is the matter?" she said. He got hold of himself, and he handed the glasses to her. "Oh my god, it's Chico," she said. He immediately went into the house and checked the batteries in the radiophone. He had reached Whitehorse before Chico got to the cabin. Arrangements were made for three men to drive from Whitehorse as far as possible up the South Canol Road. From there they would come in by snow machine. The man assured him that help would be on the way as soon as they hung up the phone.

CHAPTER 24

CHICO CAME LIMPING up to the cabin and lay at his feet. He had totally spent himself in an effort to reach home. He could not understand why his master asked him to leave his side, but he had and Chico did.

Bob knelt down to look at the harness and saw that it had definitely been cut and not broken or ripped. To Bob, this meant that Bill was alive upon releasing the animal. It also meant that he was hurt. Had he not been hurt, he'd have come home with Chico. His mind reeled as he thought of different ways he could have been hurt out there. The temperature had dropped last night. For a man with no shelter in this weather! He shuddered to think of it. Was he in a cabin? Was he lying out there alive or dead?

Tragedy has a way of bringing out a person's strengths, but often it can expose hidden weaknesses in a man's character. The latter was the case with Bob. For some unknown reason, the ugly side of his character exposed itself as he lashed out at everyone and everything for the rest of that day.

It was late in the evening when the rescue team arrived. They were cold and hungry after driving the last eighty miles by snowmobile. Any attempt at a rescue would have to wait until morning. Chico could not understand why they were so reluctant to release him so he could lead them to Bill.

Had the night not been so black, surely they'd have struck out. However, it was dark, and only fools travel in unknown territory at night. They didn't sleep that night; they tried, but there were too many thoughts crossing their minds. Chico too had a sleepless, restless night.

Bill lay in his makeshift shelter just above the location where the disaster had taken place. It was now the third night since the accident had happened. He had lost all feeling in his injured leg, and it had begun to snow. Since late afternoon he'd been dropping in and out of consciousness, and he no longer had any control over his body. At times he would shiver with the cold; at other times he felt too warm.

Right now though, he was awake and aware of the hopelessness of his situation. Bill thought about Chico then. *Did he make it home? He'd have been back by now if he didn't understand. Who am I kidding, even if he did make it, Dad's an old man. I had the only pair of snowshoes with me. It would take a young man days to walk in here.* He slipped into a deep sleep once more.

Back at the cabin, day was beginning to break. Everyone had finished breakfast, including Chico, and they nervously waited. Roger, the man in charge of the rescue, sat talking to his friends. He had decided that he and Tom would go on this one. Bob desperately wanted to be there to find Bill, but Roger had convinced him otherwise. "Bob, we don't know what we'll find out there. Hopefully Bill will be fine, but if he isn't, you are his father and . . . Well, you realize what I am saying." He did. Roy was to stay with Bob and Helen and keep trying to raise Whitehorse on the radio. After this much time, Roger wanted to have a plane sitting here in case Bill had to be transported quickly.

An hour before daylight, Roger, Tom, and Chico started across the lake. Bob, Helen, and Roy watched them until they went out of sight, then Bob turned to Helen. "Sweetheart, I owe you a big apology. There is no excuse for the way I treated everybody last night, including you. I could see that you were surprised at my actions. I was too. I suppose we never know how we'll react to a situation until we're faced with it."

"Bob, we've been together now for several years. In all that time, I have never seen you like you were last night. I don't suppose I'll ever see you that way again. If I do, I'll understand. Let's go have some coffee and help each other through this terrible wait." He took her hand, and they went inside.

It was now the morning of the fourth day. Three nights had passed since this terrible ordeal had begun. Although the mercury had plunged only one night, Bill had lain through that night with no fire. Last night too, there had been no fire, but it had snowed all day yesterday and covered the shelter with a deep blanket.

The snow continued to fall as Chico and the two men came ever closer. As strong as the dog was, he could not travel as fast as the machines. He had left the cabin leading the men, but in the interest of making better time, Roger made a decision. He felt that the dog had been smart enough to come to the cabin when his master was in trouble. Therefore, he was confident that Chico would let him know when they were approaching Bill. Once the decision was made, the men loaded the dog into the sleigh, which was being pulled by one of the machines. Chico seemed to appreciate the wisdom of this because once placed in the sleigh, he stayed there.

The threesome sped on up Big Salmon River and started across Sandy Lake. On the shore nearly two miles away, Roger could see a little cabin nestled in the trees. Upon reaching the cabin, he stopped his machine and pulled out the map that Bob had made for him. Having a clear picture of the proper course, they struck out again after checking the cabin. On they went further up the lake. The map showed a creek flowing into the lake somewhere near here. Roger kept on the alert, his eyes open to make sure they didn't miss it.

It was Tom who noticed how Chico was becoming excited. He motioned to Roger, and they stopped. Before the machines were completely stopped, Chico was off like a runaway locomotive. Each time a foot came down, his speed increased until he reached his full stride. On he flew down the lake until he reached the mouth of the creek. He then veered and went straight up the creek bed and out of sight.

The men followed the dog, now being careful to notice if the animal should leave the creek and enter the bush. They followed Chico's tracks around a bend, and then they saw it.

The snow from the whole side of the mountain had come down. God! "Nothing could have lived through that," Roger said to himself. He was convinced now that they would not find Bill alive. "That snow has to be thirty feet deep and packed," he uttered.

They reached the top and saw the remains of the moose. The ravens had kept eating on it, and now very little remained.

It was then that Chico barked; he had gone storming into Bill's snowy cocoon and was licking his master's cheek. Bill shivered a bit when the colder outside air penetrated the snow-insulated cavern. He had no way of knowing that help had arrived although he did realize that Chico had returned.

Tom, being the first aid man of the group, immediately went into action. He took only minutes to determine what Bill's injuries were. When he finished, Bill was placed in the sleigh. They wasted no time getting to the small trapline cabin where they built a fire. Tom then dressed the leg and put it in a better splint. This done, they lay Bill in the sleigh once more and continued their journey toward home. As they left the cabin, Tom felt a great respect come over him, a respect for a man and his dog. He said a silent prayer then for this man who had kept his head in a hopeless situation and had shown enormous courage as well as compassion and respect for his dogs.

The men broke out into the open and started across Big Salmon Lake. It was dark now; it had been for some time, but the snow had stopped falling, and they had followed their tracks with the headlights. Bill lay in the sleigh, wrapped in blankets under a tarp. Chico rode on the machine with Tom as they approached the light shining through the cabin window.

When they came near the cabin, Roger saw the airplane sitting on the lake, and he was glad for that. At first light, he planned to put Bill on the plane with Tom and send them to Whitehorse.

Once inside, Tom again tended to Bill's leg, which was badly swollen and deep purple from the knee down. He had cut the pant leg earlier but now completely removed it. Once Bill's underwear was cut off as well, Tom proceeded to soak the leg in cool water, all the while talking to the man who had earned his admiration. Bill lay there not knowing whether this was really happening. The last few days had produced so many hallucinations he didn't know what to believe anymore.

Later they tried to feed Bill some broth and succeeded, after a fashion. He accepted only a few spoonfuls then slipped into a deep sleep.

CHAPTER 25

THEY WOKE TO the sound of the airplane motor. Harvey, the pilot, had gone down to the water and started the engine. It could warm up while he drank his morning coffee. Bill was still sleeping when they bundled him up and took him down to the plane. Tom took care and made sure that Bill was as comfortable as possible. Before they flew off, Tom assured Helen that he would radio them that evening. With that said, the plane lifted and flew off toward the southwest, disappearing over the treetops.

Bob and Helen didn't speak much the rest of that day; they didn't have to. There is a feeling between people who truly love each other, a silent realization of each other's emotions. Helen and Bob knew that feeling and had thanked God many times for sustaining it through the years. It was time to collect their thoughts about recent events. Bob needed time to think about the future and how long Bill would be gone from them and whether in fact he would return at all. He was an old man now; it wouldn't be long until he would be unable to function out there alone. Helen knew what was going through his mind; she knew and she understood. Bob was glad for that, glad to have a woman like Helen and glad for a son like Bill—happy too because now Bill was in good hands and hopefully he would be able to return.

Tom did radio late that evening, true to his promise. Bill was in the hospital resting now, but in the morning, he was to undergo surgery. His leg had been broken in two places. Because it had frozen, the leg was in such a state of deterioration that it had to be amputated the following morning.

They wanted to be with Bill when he came out of surgery, so Tom made arrangements to have them flown to town. They stayed with Tom's parents for a week while they visited their son each day. As the week drew to a close, it was Helen who'd said, "Bob, we can't do any more good here. Bill is fine, and it will take time for his leg to heal. Let's go home. Tom and his parents are here to visit him, and they will. There is no need for us to stay any longer. The danger is over, and I'm so tired."

Before they left the hospital, the doctor told them that Bill would be sent to Vancouver in a few weeks. After an accident of this nature, it was necessary for a patient to undergo rehabilitation. Bill would also be fitted for an artificial leg, and it would be some months before he'd return. It was!

Chico missed Bill, as did his parents. For days he sat on the ledge in front of the cabin, not moving except to eat. Chico was alone now, as they were, no Bill, no dogs, and no apparent interest in what was left of his world. He could have no way of knowing what had happened since the plane carried his master away. No way of understanding that Bill was alive and doing well. Certainly he had no idea that his best friend would be back . . . someday.

They carried on through the months that followed. Winter yielded to spring, and as time passed, Chico accepted life as it now was. His enthusiasm wasn't what it had been, and some of the bounce was missing from his stride, but he was coping; Bob was glad for that. He and Chico even became friends, to a degree. Chico would now let Bob pet him, but one day he made it painfully clear that he was not to go near his head. Only one man rubbed his jowls; only one man would ever touch his head. That man was Bill.

It was on a beautiful morning in June when Tom and Harvey paid a visit. They came from the southeast with the sun at their backs. Bob and Helen heard the engine and walked out to the porch as the airplane touched down on the perfectly calm water. Chico and Bob walked down to the dock while the plane approached for mooring. As it came closer, Bob recognized the men through the window. He was anchoring the plane to the dock when the two men climbed out of their craft. He bid them welcome and shook hands. Tom dropped to one knee and began talking to Chico. "You look like you're doing fine, fella," he said. "I was talking to your boss on the phone yesterday. He asked me to bring you a friend. I have her here in the plane." When he opened the door, Chico must have caught the dog's scent because he bristled for a moment. After seeing the animal and saying their hellos, the two of them went off together to explore the surrounding area.

The rest of them went inside where Helen was removing some cinnamon buns from the oven. They sat down to coffee and buns. The conversation lasted into the late afternoon, and during the visit, they discussed many things that had bothered them over the previous months. Tom assured us that Bill was much better now. He'd been walking on his artificial leg for some time and was becoming stronger each day. Their son had been studying to become a pilot and planned to stay in Vancouver until he received his license to fly.

By the time the two men had left, Bob and Helen felt much better about the situation. They knew then that Bill had not only accepted the situation but was also prepared to deal with it. He was not only happy with life but also showing determination and the foresight to deal with his handicap. They went to bed that evening secure in the knowledge that Bill would be back in time and he would find a way to carry on.

The following morning, they concentrated on getting acquainted with the new member of the family. She was a beauty. Laika was an Alaskan malamute about two years old, rather small but heavy in the chest, had a fine mouth and large paws. Helen had named the dog Laika. She must have known how Bob had loved their first Laika though he had never said so in words.

Those two dogs got along famously right from the start. Chico maintained a certain air of aloofness with Laika, but it was plain to see that her presence made him happy once more. Hopefully this dog would shun porcupines and their quills, something the first Laika had never learned to do.

CHAPTER 26

D AWN BROKE ON a wet morning in September. It had been a restless night with many unwanted thoughts crowding Bob's mind. Memories from previous years and doubts about future years had filled his night. He had wondered whether he'd made the right decision in coming to the valley. He'd lain in bed waiting for morning. When it finally did arrive, the rain began falling on the roof just as daylight began to break. He was sitting in the kitchen when the sun began trying to peek through the dismal sky. The clouds soon thinned, and he was sure they'd have a decent day after all. The sky did clear; only a few small white puffs remained to sail over the lake. He picked up the axe that had been sitting on the porch and headed for the woodpile. He began chopping even though they had plenty of wood available for the long and possibly bitter season ahead. As the blocks of wood split and fell to the ground, so too did the doubts. Once again he knew come what may, this little piece of heaven was home and always would be.

Autumn came in a blaze of color. The valley took on a new dimension as the birds began to gather for their migration southward. He sat on the porch often then and watched the flocks of geese and ducks wing their way over the cabin. The squirrels too were busy gathering cones and preparing themselves for the months ahead. He'd sat there day after day, content in the knowledge that this year they were well prepared for whatever was to come.

It was Helen who suggested that they decorate a tree for Christmas. He agreed, feeling that maybe a tree was needed to lift their spirits. It had been almost thirteen months since the accident. Bill had been lucky, lucky on many counts, not the least of which had been the obedience and love of Chico. He shivered when he thought of what might have happened. There had been no Christmas tree last year, no celebration, just prayers of thanks and quick recovery for their son.

The day before Christmas began much like any winter day in the north. They awoke to a cold cabin; the fire had gone out during the night. Bob lay there for a moment, not wanting to brave the cold floor with his bare feet. Then Helen stirred, and he knew that she would get up if he didn't, so he threw the covers aside. He shivered as he lighted the fire; he felt a draft behind him. Turning around, he saw that the door was ajar. As he walked over to close it, Laika whined, and then he saw her huddled in the corner beside the kitchen table. She had come in during the night for some unknown reason and was lying there quietly. Bob walked over to her then, hoping that she hadn't been hurt. It was then that he saw the three little bundles of fur. Three puppies had been born while they slept, and he hadn't even known that Laika was about to give birth.

Helen had known, however; apparently, she'd been watching over Laika these last weeks like a mother hen with chicks. She heard Bob talking to Laika in the kitchen and immediately got out of bed. They could not understand why she had come inside the cabin to whelp. She had though, and now Helen hurried about in an effort to make Laika as comfortable as possible. She went to the closet in the bedroom and took out a blanket, then laid it on the floor. While Laika decided whether or not to accept the bed, Helen and Bob proceeded to get dressed. That done, they sat down to a cup of coffee before making breakfast. As the cabin began to heat up, Bob noticed that Laika began to pant a bit. He realized then that she was not going to be able to stay inside for long. A dog like her who's been raised outdoors cannot cope with a heated cabin for long. After breakfast, he planned to build her and her puppies an adequate doghouse.

When Bob had eaten, he went outside, and Chico was standing at the door. He had come down from the ledge and couldn't fully understand what was going on. He just stood there with a questioning look on his face, an expression that almost asked, "Why is Laika in the cabin? What is she doing there? Is she all right?"

He put Bob in mind of an expectant father, pacing back and forth and worrying about something. Something he knows he has no control over. There were few times in Chico life's where he had little or no control in the situation or its outcome. This was one of those times.

Bob had almost finished Laika's new house when he heard an airplane off in the distance. The sound was muffled at first, and then it slowly became clearer. As the plane came into sight, it was obvious that they were about to have company.

The plane circled a few times looking for a smooth snow surface to set down on. After making a decision, the pilot landed the plane quite a distance away then began skiing toward the cabin.

"Put the coffee on, Helen. We've got company," Bob yelled.

"I'm way ahead of you, Bob. I've prayed for this for weeks. Just a minute and I'll walk down with you."

They were both standing on the dock when the plane came to a stop. The pilot's door opened, and Harvey climbed out. Bob could see from the smile on his face that the visit was to be of a jovial nature. The thought had crossed Bob's mind that maybe this was to be a bearing of more bad news, but the smile convinced him otherwise.

"Merry Christmas," Harvey said as he grabbed a bag and started to walk around to the dock.

"Merry Christmas to you too, Harvey. We certainly didn't expect to see you out here at this time of year."

"Well, normally, I wouldn't be, but Bill wanted me to bring you two some Christmas presents, and I'm just an old softy."

"You have heard from Bill then. How is he making out?"

"Why don't you ask him yourself, Bob?"

"What!"

The passenger's door opened, and Bill poked his head around the edge of the door.

What happened next would bring a tear to the hardest heart.

Helen saw him first. She didn't speak; she cried. She had held in her loneliness and deep feelings for many months. Each person who bears a terrible hurt bears it in a different way. Her way had been to hold in all the pain and frustration in an attempt to make things easier for Bob. As she approached her son, she quivered; Helen ran down the dock, peering through tear-filled eyes, and reached her son as he stepped out of the plane. She had needed a good cry for months; now that Bill was home and safe, she let her pent-up emotions free and sobbed for some time. Bill held his mother, kissing her cheek and comforting her. He realized that Helen deserved this, needed the release, and he waited patiently until his mother regained her former poise.

Once Helen had composed herself, she turned to Bob.

"I'm sorry, Bob, not for becoming emotional and not for being the first to hug our son, but sorry for taking up so much of his time when I know you're aching to hold him too."

"There's no need to be sorry for loving somebody, Helen. I didn't realize that you were holding so much feeling within you. Thank God you've been able to get it out. I would like to welcome the boy too," he cried.

"Let's go up to the cabin and get out of the cold," Helen said.

"We will, Mom, but we aren't finished here yet."

The airplane door opened, and a young lady climbed out. Bill walked down the dock and took her by the hand.

"Mom, Dad, I'd like you to meet my wife, Donna." Helen's eyes went glassy as she walked over and kissed her daughter-in-law on the cheek.

In the excitement of the homecoming, Harvey had stood to one side and watched. He too had a tear in his eye when they asked him to come up for coffee.

"No, thanks, you people enjoy this moment. I won't take any of your time this trip. I must get back to Whitehorse early. I have a meeting with Tom. We'll return in a few days with more to talk about."

The four of them stood on the dock and watched until the plane went out of sight, then they went up to the cabin.

Chico was sitting on the ledge when they came up the path. As they approached the cabin, he became uneasy. He didn't seem to know who these intruders were, but obviously they were welcomed by Helen and Bob, so he settled down. Bill called to him then.

"Chico, come here, fella, come see who's come home." Bill knelt down on one knee and began talking to the dog.

"What's wrong, fella? Have you forgotten about me?"

At the sound of Bill's voice, Chico raised his ears. He began to approach slowly. As he came closer, he began to sniff the air, trying to get some hint of a scent. He came ever closer until he could smell the man who seemed so friendly. Somewhere he had known the scents he now smelled, but there was something different.

"Come here, boy. It's Bill. I've come home to stay, home to those I love, home to Mom and Pop, home to you, you wonderful dog."

The girls were standing on the porch when everything came together in Chico's mind. The scent, the voice, the tenderness formed a picture, a picture of his master. He came on a dead run; he and Bill rolled over and over in the snow. Chico was whining and Bill was crying. For the first time, Chico was wagging his tail. It had been beneath his dignity before, but now even he forgot dignity for a time. Bob stood to one side with a lump in his throat and thought, *Seldom has there been a bond like this between man and animal.* It was obvious that Chico was as happy to have Bill home as they were. For hours he lay at Bill's feet by the kitchen table. Chico had never been allowed inside the cabin before. He became uneasy once he remembered this; the heat too began to bother him, and he went outside with Laika and her puppies. Laika had taken up residence in her new home now. She had gained some confidence and assurance in her ability to handle the responsibility of caring for her first litter of puppies.

Night approached and folded around a family that was united once again. Helen said thank-you for bringing her son back to her. She said special thanks too for his wife, whom she already came to like. It would be much easier now with female companionship, easier and more appealing, much more appealing. They went to bed. It had been a busy day, an emotionally tiring day.

CHAPTER 27

B OB AWOKE CHRISTMAS morning to the smell of pancakes in the room. Helen and Donna were up and talking about how she and Bill had met first at university then met again after Bill's operation. She was a nurse then and was employed at the rehabilitation center. The two became very close over the months. When Bill decided to return to their valley, he asked Donna to come with him as his wife. It had been a big decision to make, and it was not made overnight. Donna had always been infatuated by the thought of living away from the crowds and concrete jungle, but she had never believed that the opportunity would present itself. When it did, she admitted to being frightened by it. She was more frightened, however, by the fear of being separated from her man. She loved Bill very much and would never be without him. If being with the man she'd come to love so very much meant leaving her roots behind, then that's what she'd do. She knew that she'd follow Bill to the ends of the earth if need be. Bob could see the admiration in Helen's eyes then for this lady who had come into their lives. Bill knew too how lucky he was. He showed it in many ways, little things most people wouldn't notice, but Donna did notice. She knew from his actions, the respect, the open affection, and his touch of tenderness that she had acquired the love of a good man, a love that knew no boundaries, a love that few people ever know. She knew it and was thankful for it. She welcomed the challenge that life would present and knew that her life would undoubtedly be tough but the good times would outweigh the bad. Through it all, they would be together, living and loving as nature intended.

Christmas Day passed amid good food and even better conversation. The months came and went, and soon it was spring. Bill and his father worked the time away building a new home for the newlyweds. Bob was surprised to see his son work the way he did in spite of his artificial leg. He had to use more intuition and forethought when lifting heavy loads now, but lift them he did. For the most part, he was as handy a man now as he'd ever been. Soon the cabin would be finished, and he could move his wife into their new home. Bob had to admit that things would be better then. Four people required more room than was available in their small cabin.

They talked more of the accident in the final days of construction. Bill wanted to return to Brown Creek after the ice went out. He had a need to be close once more to the site where he'd lost the animals he'd loved, close to the spot where he'd almost lost his life.

When the time was right, they prepared for an overnight trip to the slide location. They left early one morning in a canoe. Bill, Bob, and Chico started across the lake just as the sun began to rise. They planned to do some fishing as they made their way across the lake. It was not to be a hurried trip but rather an opportunity for Bill to get back in touch with the wild. Bill felt that he must do this small thing before he could go on with his life. There were many thoughts in his mind that were not clear. Maybe, by returning, he could fill in the memory gaps of the ordeal. Maybe, by returning to the creek, he would find clues that would help him to fully understand what had happened; maybe not, but he had to try.

They arrived at the line cabin early in the afternoon. Bill began cleaning the fish they'd caught while Bob rustled up some wood and started a fire. When they had eaten, the day was still young. Bill looked at his dad and said, "Do you feel like going farther today? It's not far now. We could get there and back before dark."

Bob could tell that Bill was impatient; he wanted to get it over with. His father agreed to go.

When they arrived at the location where Bill's brush with death had occurred, they got out of the canoe. Bill combed the area for signs that would help him remember. They found what was left of his makeshift shelter. On the far bank, there were a few bones on the ground, remains of the two wolves he had shot. He searched the water but found nothing. It was now the second spring since the accident happened. The ice would surely have carried the sleigh out to the lake. After sitting for a while and thinking, Bill decided that they would return to the line cabin for the night. There was nothing lying around that would jog his memory. While climbing into the canoe, he noticed something lying on the bottom of the creek. Whatever it was, it was worth checking, he thought. He then waded into the creek and reached down to pick up whatever it was he'd seen. Once he grasped the object, he made a hasty retreat for the shore. He was standing there shaking the cold off and trying to get the circulation back into his leg when Bob walked up.

"This stump is good for something after all, Dad. At least the cold water doesn't bother it. Boy, that water's cold."

He then knelt down and picked up his rifle. It was rusted and would never be usable again. He wanted to keep it though, and he laid it in the canoe.

They reached the line cabin before Bill uttered a word. When he did talk, he tried to explain to his dad what it was that had baffled him about his ordeal.

"You see, Dad, it was days after I arrived at the hospital before I awoke. When I did wake up, it took me quite some time to realize that I was truly alive. I was in limbo, I suppose, but I distinctly remember pulling the trigger of my rifle after lying in that lean-to for days. Lying there with the pain as long as I did must have made me delirious. I was convinced that I'd ended it. From then on, I remembered nothing until I awoke with nurses running around, doctors coming and going. I didn't know what to believe. I was sure that I'd killed myself. I was certain that I'd had the rifle with me in the lean-to. When I found it in the creek, I realized that my mind had played a trick on me. It couldn't possibly be in both places. Obviously I only thought it had been with me. I knew of course that there had to be an explanation, and I had to try and find it.

"If I'd have found the rifle when I tried to dig the dogs out, if I'd have had it with me in the lean-to, my life would have ended there. Thank God my mind played a trick on me. Thankfully my lower leg is all I lost."

They spent the night in the line cabin, and when morning arrived, they returned home.

CHAPTER 28

LATE SPRING SAW Bill begin to work again. He started close to home, then slowly his range became larger. In time his trips spanned two to three days, but never did he stay more than two nights. Bill always left his parents a rough map of the area he planned to prospect and always took Chico with him.

By fall, the medical bills were paid. Bill and Donna made a trip to Whitehorse for material and other supplies. Donna wanted to make drapes for their home. When they returned, Tom was with them. He would spend a few days hunting and fishing. Tom also had business to talk over with Bill.

That evening they sat and talked. Tom asked Bob to sit in with them and offer his opinions of Tom's planned endeavor.

"Bill, you and I have been friends for some time, good friends. Don't take what I am about to say in a derogatory way. You know that I don't mean to hurt your feelings."

"Go on, Tom."

"You're doing fine now, Bill. You've done a fine job over the summer with your prospecting."

"I'm listening. What is your point?"

"Just this, winter is coming. We both know that it will be much harder to get around on snowshoes than it has been on hard ground. I know that you will do it because you are what you are. Will you be able to do it ten years from now or fifteen?"

"I can understand what you're saying, Tom, and I agree. Where are you trying to take me with this conversation?"

"I have always wanted to do what you are doing. I believe I've come up with a way to do that. I need your help, Bill. Will you give it to me? Can you and I be partners in this valley?"

"What kind of a harebrained scheme are you hatching in that head of yours?"

"Fishing trips, Bill, fishing trips. You've noticed that there are more and more canoeists passing by each year. Instead of mumbling under your breath at them, why don't we use their presence to our advantage?"

"I can see what you're getting at, Tom, but those people wouldn't pay us to take them fishing. My god, man, if they get here by themselves, why would they need us?"

"They don't, Bill, but for every person who has the knowledge and ability to travel this watershed, there must be ten who don't. Ten people who would love to have an opportunity to witness the beauty here and live within that beauty for a while."

"Do you have any idea what the cost would be for a project like that? Tom, I don't have much cash."

"I've been in contact with people from the Federal Development Bank. They come to Whitehorse periodically, and I have worked out an agreement in principle with them. I have enough money to get us started."

"Then why do you need me?"

"Bill, the whole deal hinges on you. You know the area. You have most of the needed facilities here. You and your dad are to be involved, or the bank won't go along with the idea. We need your trapline to make this thing work. You have cabins every ten miles up and down the river. We can use them for fly camps and overnight lodging. The possibilities are endless. Really, the only great expense we'll have is building a lodge."

Bill thought hard about the proposal. Bob could see from his expression that he was intrigued with the idea. He was very interested but at the same time frightened by the whole idea. Hospital bills were the only experience he'd had with credit and all the nightmares it could bring. Bob felt that it was time to say something.

"Boys, if I am to be a part of this, I am going to have some input toward it. I won't be able to offer much help away from home, so we'll build the lodge right here. I can certainly be of some assistance in that capacity. We won't need the bank. Before we came to live here, Bill's mother and I sold our home. We owned that house, and we've never needed the money. It's sitting in the bank in Whitehorse. I can't think of a better use for the money than this. I would like to assure you that I am all for this idea of yours, Tom. It's time we stopped being selfish about this land of ours. The time is right to assist others in enjoying some of the wonders we have known here. Let's do it and the sooner the better.

"We won't get rich doing this, but we'll be doing what we love to do. We'll make a comfortable living, and if it takes off the way it may, well, that'll be a bonus. What do you think, Bill?"

"In light of the fact that we won't have to borrow money to get it off the ground, yes, I'm in, but I think we should still talk to the bank. The way I see it, the whole operation is going to hinge on quick access to and from Whitehorse. I have a valid pilot's license, and we need a plane. If we can get a loan to buy one, we are home free. We'll have to approach Harvey about flying for us until I can receive a commercial license. After that, we can run it ourselves."

They formed a company the following week. Bill, Tom, and Bob became equal partners in Big Salmon Tours, and a new way of life began on the shore of this lake they regard as theirs.

In the weeks that followed, Bill and Tom were gone much of the time. They had business to attend to, documents to sign, and a plane to buy. When they did return to begin the construction of the lodge, they flew in with Harvey. Bill hadn't been able to find a suitable plane for their needs at a reasonable cost. There were two new ones that had interested him, but the prices were unreasonable. They decided that for the present, they'd use Harvey's charter service. It would be at least a year before they could seriously consider booking any fishing parties anyway. For at least that long then, Harvey would be contacted on the radio, and he would bring them any supplies they might need.

They sat down then, and after much thought, they devised a blueprint of sorts. Plans are much easier to change with a pencil than with a shovel. With that in mind, they put aside one idea after another until they could come up with a design suitable to them all. They conceived such a plan late one afternoon and were so pleased with themselves, they proceeded to have a few drinks. One led to another, and soon they were feeling no pain. That was the only time Bill was ever to see his mother take a drink. She had never learned how to handle alcohol; there was no need to, and she very seldom used it. That night though, there seemed to be something bothering Helen; she needed a form of release. The rye provided that for her, and before she realized it, she had consumed far too much. They put her to bed early that night, and the following morning she was sick.

CHAPTER 29

THEY LEARNED THEN that she hadn't been feeling well for days. Donna spent a good part of the morning talking to her and decided that they should take Helen to Whitehorse for a checkup. Bill contacted Harvey and asked him to fly out. He told him what the problem was and that Donna suspected appendicitis. Harvey came and left with Helen; Donna went with them too. She wanted to be with her mother-in-law in case any problems developed.

They didn't expect any trouble; after all, people had their appendix removed every day.

Donna radioed the following day; she was crying. Bill talked to her. "I won't be back until tomorrow, hon. I have a few arrangements to make here before I bring Mom home."

"What's wrong, dear? Why are you crying?"

"Mom had a stroke on the operating table, Bill. Things were going so well until then. She's gone, Bill. Mom passed away an hour ago."

"Damn these radiophones," Bill said to himself.

Bob was with Bill during this time. He heard the conversation and sat in disbelief.

"Dad, I'm sorry you had to hear about Mom's death this way. I wish I could have made this easier somehow."

Laika came up to the porch then and rubbed herself against Bob's pants. She had become very close to Bob since her first litter of pups were born. Often she would do something, anything to attract his attention and, in turn, his affection. He did love this dog, and even now in spite of his sorrow, a hand went down and began rubbing her neck tenderly. Bill walked up to the porch, and Bob Walker's mind came away from past events to concentrate on the present once more.

Bill and Donna were worried about their father. To grieve a lost loved one is of course natural, but Bob had stopped eating and sleeping. Laika was the only one that he seemed to care about. Even his appearance had changed; it seemed he'd aged ten years over the ten days since Helen was buried.

The Bible says that the Lord never sends us more sorrow than we can bear; Bill was beginning to doubt that promise. He tried to understand, and he was sure he could help if only his father would speak. If only he would try to communicate some of the sorrow he held inside. He seemed to be in a trance, a state of disbelief. Bill felt, given time, his father would improve. He also knew that Bob must admit to himself that Helen was gone. Until he did that, there would continue to be a cause for concern.

In the weeks that followed, Bob did begin to rally, slowly at first, and then came a marked change in his attitude. He continued to have bad days, yes, but in time he learned to deal with the memories that kept coming back to haunt him.

There came a morning when a knock was heard on Bill's door. He opened the door, and his father was standing there, a smile on his face and a coffee pot in his hand.

"I came for breakfast."

Bill smiled, and life continued in spite of their loss.

CHAPTER 30

BILL AND TOM were more than happy to have Bob back to consistently help with construction once more. They were in the process of cutting down the logs they needed for the construction of the lodge. Earlier they had gone into Teslin and purchased a tractor, which they were using to move the logs from the beach to a pile near where the lodge was to be built. The logs would remain piled for one full year, in which time they would dry. Seasoning would guard against future splits and warps in the wood, which would spell disaster.

Moving the tractor to the homesite had been an experience in itself. From Teslin, they merely drove the machine up the South Canol Road. They came north approximately sixty-five miles, then followed a makeshift access road that led to the lake. Once they arrived at the lake, they had a major problem. The problem was that from where they stood, it was still at least eight miles to the cabins. They had to build a barge large enough to buoy the weight of the machine and themselves through the water, which was quite shallow at the point of loading. Once through the shallows, the lake's depths plunged to darkness. It was necessary then to construct a raft from logs large enough to float the weight yet small enough to avoid being hung up on the sandy bottom. Needless to say, the two men did not brag about their plan; they put it into action and hoped for the best. Once the raft was built, they waited for a calm day.

Three days later, the calm day arrived. A ramp was built out to deep water. They positioned the raft at the end of the ramp and anchored it. Bill drove the tractor out onto the ramp. When the front wheels rolled onto the raft, it began to tip.

"Get clear, Tom. Here I come."

The wheels rolled to the middle of the raft, and it leveled out. The weight of the tractor was now on the raft. It settled down into the water and left a space, which the back wheels would have to drop to. This was the critical point. Then Tom cut some logs of the proper lengths. These he put lengthwise from the bottom of the raft to the bottom of the lake. That done, Bill drove the machine fully onto the raft.

"We did it, Bill. Scared the hell out of me, but we did it."

"Yes, we did, didn't we? We aren't home yet though. Get in that canoe, and start pulling. Take it slow and hope the rope doesn't break. I'll pray that the wind doesn't come up."

The weather cooperated, and with the help of the outboard motor and the square-stern freighter canoe, they got the tractor to the cabin. They built another ramp, took another chance, and moved that machine up onto the beach.

By the time Bob came back to work, most of the trees had been felled. They had cut these trees from a sidehill that sloped to the river, upstream from the lake. Once they limbed the trees, they then rolled them down the hill and into the river. The river carried the logs to the lake, and the freighter canoe pulled them across the lake to the cabin.

Once the logs were piled, Tom went back to Whitehorse. He returned often in the year that followed to visit and to check the condition of the logs, which were so essential to the whole plan.

When the geese began to fly over the cabin once more, Tom returned. He brought with him all his personal possessions as well as the proper tools that would be needed to begin construction. They began to work on the lodge first, wanting to complete the jobs in order of preference. The lodge was surely the biggest task and the most important.

Over the years, Bob had become a craftsman in the art of hewing logs. Much time and labor was saved through his ability to make the perfect cuts needed to pile log onto log as the lodge slowly took shape. It had meant much more effort on Bob's part to dovetail the corners. Effort or no, being a stickler for detail, he would make that extra effort. As the structure began to rise toward the sky, it was perfectly obvious that he had been right. He was proud of his handiwork and rightly so; the lodge was becoming a thing of beauty.

In the evenings, being by himself a great deal, Bob began to rekindle an old love, a love for composition in verse. He had long admired men of poetry and the mastery of using descriptive words in rhyme to express an idea. He enjoyed the works of many poets over the years, and naturally, like others, he had his favorites.

Bob always loved reading about the Yukon; perhaps that was one reason why he was drawn to the works of a man who'd loved this land as he did. He could relate to works like "The Law of the Yukon," "The Shooting of

Dan McGrew," and "The Cremation of Sam McGee." They were among his favorites. He spent hours reading and attempting to write. So far he'd been unsuccessful, but he'd go on trying. He was not a dreamer; he knew he would never rival the work of Robert Service, but one good verse would be nice.

Between working in earnest on the lodge all day and reading well into the evening, time passed quickly for Bob. Bill was thankful for this because it made his life easier as well. He no longer worried about his father's frame of mind, and that in itself helped a great deal.

It was well into spring when Bob decided that they all needed a day off. The ice was gone from the river now, and he felt a yen for a fishing trip. "I don't care how long we stay or even if we catch any fish. It's a lovely day, we've been working too hard, and we deserve a day of enjoyment." Needless to say, they all agreed with him. As work progressed on the lodge, they were becoming obsessed with the idea that it must be finished quickly. Such was not the case at all. They were far ahead of the timetable they had set for themselves.

Yesterday had been a bad day from the start. Early in the afternoon, Tom had almost been hurt. They decided that the pace was going to have to slow down. They'd been working too hard and too long. Patience was beginning to suffer, and they were becoming sarcastic with one another.

So go fishing they did. An enjoyable day was spent in an effort to expel the tension and aggravation that had been building through the months. Little did they realize when they came off the lake late in the evening that they had learned a valuable lesson that day. From that day forward, when one or more of them felt a need for detachment from the situation, they'd go off by themselves, go off to be alone until thoughts were collected and pressures were released. Even the best of friends must realize that personalities will clash if confined together too long.

It was then that Tom began going into Whitehorse periodically. His parents were aging, as everyone does, and he wanted to spend more time with them. Living in the valley with Helen now gone and the others impressed upon him that the love of his parents would not be available forever. He'd watched Bill and his father; he could appreciate the love and respect that was a bond between the two. Tom and his dad had not experienced any such feeling of comradeship. Living in the city demanded that a man spend a lot of time away from home. Tom's father had been a government employee whose job entailed much traveling; there had been little time for the two to become as close as he would have liked. Now, however, his dad was retired, and he decided to really make an effort to become closer friends and to try and understand the man he loved so very much.

During one of these visits to Whitehorse, he bumped into Wendy. They had gone to school together, graduated, and then went their separate ways. Wendy had left the Yukon to further her education and then returned to work in Whitehorse. She was a social worker now with a degree in psychology and enjoyed working with people. She took pride in her job and therefore excelled at it. As time went on, Wendy and Tom began to date, and he spent as much time as possible with her.

The summer quickly passed, and it became evident that they had to stop work on the lodge for a while. Winter was just around the corner, and previous experience had taught them a lesson about early preparation for the season. The lodge was closed in now, the roof was completed, and all the windows were mounted. Tomorrow they would set the exterior doors in place; the rest would have to wait until after the hunt.

CHAPTER 31

BILL DECIDED THAT they would hunt in the Sandy Lake area first. There was a moose lick close to the river. Last fall the animals hadn't been using it, but he remembered seeing several moose in the area during this past year. Hopefully they had come back to it now; that would certainly make their job easier.

Bill and Tom started across the lake early the following afternoon. They intended to go as far as the line cabin on Sandy Lake that evening. At the cabin, they would be right in the hunting area early in the morning. Previous years had taught them that early morning was the best time to hunt these animals—early in the morning just before the sun came up, when mist rose from the water, which was warmer than the air over it at that time of day. If there was an animal in the area, chances were he would be standing in water up to his knees, his head beneath the water eating tender plants that have been newly grown during the course of the summer.

The men knew that within a week or two, early-morning frost would cause the still sloughy water to freeze. At such time, the moose would begin to leave their summer eating grounds and seek higher ground. By doing this, they would avoid breaking through the thin layers of ice. Those that do break the ice often cut their legs, and then they too realize that the soft summer way must yield to a harsher method of sustaining their lives. Bill learned many things from his father about this animal, not the least of which was the fact that just when you think you've figured them out, they'll do something entirely against their nature. In light of that fact, Bill never tried to outthink the moose. He just used his experience with them and hunted according to a law of averages based on that experience. He felt that this ritual of leaving the water in autumn signaled the coming of the rut to this animal. During this time of year, the big bulls began to come down from the mountains where they spent the summer to escape from the flies. Soon the valley would be full of grunts and snorts, bangs and crashes as the bulls would fight and vie for the affection of as many cows as possible. Moose would stop eating until the rut was over. This meant that their bodies would have to rely on fat reserves built up during the summer. It also meant, to Bill, that the animals would toughen as they sought one another out, traveling miles across country calling to each other in their quest to reproduce. Bill knew the ways of this animal; he knew too that now they were in the best physical condition they'd enjoy all year. *Now is the proper time*, he thought as the men kept moving ever closer to the line cabin.

They came around one of the many islands that dot the water in Big Salmon Lake. When they broke out into the clear once more, Tom raised his rifle. Bill put his hand on Tom's arm and applied enough pressure to stop Tom from taking a bead on what was the most beautiful rack of horns that Tom had ever seen.

"What the hell are you doing, Bill? That moose is all the meat we'll need for the whole winter."

"We don't need him bad enough, Tom. There'll be others, and rest assured we will see others."

Tom couldn't understand Bill's actions, but he respected the man. He knew there was a reason, and he knew that it would be explained. He didn't push his point of view, but he wasn't happy with the situation either.

There was a short peninsula that reached out into the lake. On one side of this strip of ground, the river flowed into Big Salmon; on the other side, more of the lake, which continued up the small valley for a few miles. The moose was standing out on the tip of this stretch of narrow ground, watching their approach. As they came closer, he walked down into the river water, swam across, and stood on the other side. The animal watched them for a few seconds, then slipped into the trees and was gone.

Tom was still shaking his head as the freighter canoe started up the river. A few more miles and they'd pass the slough where Bill planned to concentrate his efforts the following day. Beyond that, they'd come to a point where the river became even wider until it merged with Sandy Lake.

Upon reaching the cabin, the men unloaded the canoe. Bill was peeling potatoes in preparation for their evening meal when Tom spoke.

"I think you owe me an explanation, Bill. I'm trying to be patient, but damn, I wanted that bull."

"Tom, I believe that if we look after nature, she'll look after us. We don't need meat bad enough to shoot an animal like that.

"I've spent the major part of my life in this valley, and I've learned many things from my father, Tom. I've also learned a lot from an even better teacher than he is. Nature has taught me that we are only a small portion of a grand design. We are no more important or less significant than any of God's other creatures. In other parts of the world, people can make mistakes. They can go on making one blunder after another and get by because there are others to pack them. In this land, many times, to err is to die. If a man is lucky, he has a friend to lean on, and even then, he must be careful. A mistake made by that friend can mean his undoing.

"I have had a great respect for the wolf since I was a child. They are efficient hunters. They show a strong allegiance to their leader and to the rest of the pack. Like us, they choose mates and very often remain together for life. I suppose the single thing I admire most about the animal is the fact that they kill to live. They do not live to kill. They kill when they must and then stay near the carcass until it is completely eaten. Only then do they hunt again, if necessary."

"What does this have to do with shooting a bull moose?"

"Tom, tell me, what did you see when you looked at that animal earlier?"

"I saw the most beautiful moose I have ever seen in my life. I saw a rack of horns that would extend from one side of the lodge's fireplace to the other. I saw a chance to shoot our winter's supply of meat right beside the water. In very little time, we could have loaded it into our canoe and been on our way home. What did you see?"

"I saw a beautiful animal, yes, but I saw more than that. To me, that moose represents an animal in his peak. Being in his peak, he signifies, to me, much more than just one animal. His presence means five, maybe ten healthy calves in the spring. Those calves may not be born if we destroy the possibility. In his absence, a lesser bull may win the right to reproduce his kind. If so, the species will be weakened.

"There are many moose in this valley, Tom. We'll see others. I like to take a lone two-year-old bull, an animal who doesn't figure in the mating game. Such an animal will provide all the meat we need, and by killing such a moose, we remove only one life from the scheme of things. I can live with that."

"I never thought of it that way, Bill. I suppose, if the truth were known, I just didn't think. Thanks for bringing me with you, and I will always remember what you just said."

They sat down to eat by the light that was coming from the heater. As the wood burned inside, the beam of light glowed through the glass in the door and illuminated the cabin to a degree. They discussed many things as they sat and finished their meal. When they did finish, the dishes were washed, and they retired. Five o'clock comes early!

As dawn began to break, the two men were sitting quietly amid the trees overlooking the full length of the small slough that lay below them. They'd left the canoe on the riverbank and walked slowly up the hill to a narrow ridge that skirted one side of this marsh. Below them now was a thick cloud, a mist that would soon begin to abate as the sun's rays heated the air above the now-warmer water beneath it. They sat on a dead fall, deathlike. They hoped that beneath the fog, there'd be a moose standing. If so, the trip would end shortly, and soon they could resume work on the lodge, which had become a source of great pride in both their minds.

When the fog did lift, Bill shrugged his shoulders, "We can't win every time, Tom."

"No, that's a fact. What'll we do now?"

Bill smiled, wondering himself what to do next. "Let's walk up the hill a bit farther. There's a lick up here always. It won't do any good to sit on it now, but we should find out if they've been using it."

They followed an old game trail that led toward the moose lick. Bill was thinking that there was no hope of finding much sign because the trail appeared unused. As they approached the lick, however, the old game trail merged with another. This one had definitely been used a great deal—and recently. When they reached the lick, it became obvious that moose were using it. The whole area had been trampled with fresh signs. There had been at least four animals here last night, maybe five.

It was then that Tom noticed the sticks that were spiked to a large tree forming a makeshift ladder that rose up to a platform, high above the lick. Up above, there were two cross braces, which spanned the distance between two trees. Atop these cross braces lay the boards that made up the vantage point from where two men could watch over the area. Animals coming into the lick are unable to smell a man when he sits up above this way. Bill and his father had erected this stand years ago. Their idea being that if they must shoot a moose for winter meat, and they must, then shoot the animal that will have the least detrimental effect on nature. The stand supplied a means for Bill and his father to pick and choose the animals that were to be destroyed. Bill was happy to see that the years had not destroyed the platform. He and Tom would use it this night.

When the men reached the canoe once more, they set it into the river. As they started across Sandy Lake, Bill looked at Tom and winked.

"I hope you've got a strong back. You're going to need it tomorrow."

"I'm looking forward to it, Bill. Packing a whole moose that far will be tough. It'll take time, but I'll do it."

"You'll do it! Can't I help?"

"Bill, you're quite a guy, your intentions are good, but how are you going to pack a quarter of moose meat over half a mile of forest floor with one leg?"

"Sometimes I believe that you are an incurable skeptic. I may have a bum leg, but there's nothing wrong with my head that I know of."

"I don't know what you've got planned, but I'm looking forward to it, almost as much as pulling the trigger when you tell me which moose I can shoot."

"It's late now, Tom. What say we go back to the cabin, get a bite to eat, and prepare for tonight? The moose will be lying down now anyway, and they won't begin to move again until late this afternoon. We'll come back this evening and sit in our tree house."

"Sounds good to me. I'm hungry enough to eat a muskrat."

"That's good! That's what you'll be eating."

They reached the cabin and then proceeded to muster up a meal. After they had eaten, Tom began to read his first aid manual. Bill went outside to the canoe and returned with a large piece of moose hide. It had been saved from a previous hunt. The hair had been removed, and it would now be used as a thick substitute for the leather he now wished for but did not have. He began to work with the hide while sitting at the table. He cut narrow strips from the skin, which he intended to use later when he would fashion a travois of sorts to aid him in transporting the meat. He chuckled as he thought of what Tom had said earlier.

"Your intentions are good, but how are you going to be able to pack a quarter of moose meat over half a mile of forest floor with only one leg?" Ha! Little does Tom realize that even he is not strong enough to accomplish a feat like that in spite of his two good legs.

Tom looked up from his book.

"What are you chuckling about now? I swear, sometimes I wonder if you have more fun in your thoughts than you do in reality."

Bill never answered; he went on working with the hide, whistling and chuckling away to himself.

Tom realized that he was not going to be enlightened as to Bill's thoughts, so he returned to reading his book.

As the afternoon wore on, Bill, having completed his task, turned to Tom, who was awaking from a short nap.

"If you can get your act together, we should head out."

"Don't worry about me. I'm ready when you are."

They wrapped what was left of the muskrat meat in a cloth, put it in a knapsack along with some moose jerky, and left the cabin.

About an hour before sundown, they reached the moose lick. Tom climbed the ladder first with the knapsack on his back. They'd brought a rope with them; this was dropped down to Bill, who tied it to Tom's rifle. Once the rifles plus the piece of hide were hoisted up, Bill began to scale the ladder. It was a slow process at first. By using his arms to lift the weight of his body, he was able to let his bad leg dangle free while supporting his weight with his good one. He adjusted quickly to this method, and soon Bill was also atop the platform.

They were sitting, chewing on jerky, just at dusk, when the first noise was heard. A short distance away, a twig snapped, very little noise, but enough. Bill heard it; he understood immediately what it was. He then raised a finger to his lips in an effort to ensure Tom's silence. A few minutes later, they came out of the trees. A cow and two calves, thinking the area was safe, came into the clearing that was the lick. Here they would stay for a short time obtaining the growth-promoting and body-sustaining minerals that came so close to the ground's surface. Little did they know that overhead sat two men who may very well be their instrument of death.

Tom looked over at Bill, and a smile crossed his lips. He made a gesture toward the moose, and then Bill shook his head. Tom settled back, rested against the tree, and went on watching the animals.

Bill thought then that it may be foolish to let these animals go. There were no assurances that the men would see more, but still he remembered what his father had told him so many times.

"One animal, Bill. The one that will have the least affect for the perfect balance."

The calves were too small, and the cow represented one, maybe two calves come spring. The animals loitered for a half hour or so, then entered the trees and went down the hill toward the river.

The men continued to sit; their backs were sore now from all the sitting. They didn't dare stand up and stretch lest the platform collapse and they fall to the ground. The moon was out now; it clearly illuminated the clearing below them. Bill was about to call a halt to their wait and leave when he heard another noise. It seemed to come from far up the hill. Whatever it was, it certainly wasn't concerned with being quiet. As it approached, it made less and less noise until they heard nothing for a time. The minutes passed, and nothing. Bill knew what was going on, or at least he was sure he knew. There was a moose out there, a crafty fella who had learned to be patient. He would come in when he was ready, and in the meantime, Bill would wait though his back muscles were demanding to be stretched. Then a scuffle and a scrape nearer to their position, and Bill knew then that there was more than one animal nearby. One of these he felt was a mature bull; he hoped the other would not be. A dry cow then showed herself at the far end of the lick. The big bull shortly appeared directly under the two men. Last but not least, the culprit responsible for all the noise appeared in front of their position. The two men looked down on these monarchs of the north woods, obviously in awe at the sight of them. Bill lifted a hand and touched Tom's coat sleeve. He pointed to the young three-point bull; Tom raised his rifle. Bill waited until he heard a report from Tom's firearm, saw the animal go down, and then Tom lowered his gun and watched as the other two disappeared into the darkness.

The two men then proceeded to dress the moose, and when they'd finished, they walked down the hill toward the river. They would return tomorrow after a good night's rest to quarter the animal and pack it out of the bush.

Morning came, and the sky was clear. The men were thankful for the fine weather; it would make the task before them much more pleasant.

When they arrived at the lick, the two men proceeded to quarter the carcass that lay in the lick. When that was done, Bill helped Tom lift one of the quarters to Tom's shoulder. Tom started gingerly down the hill toward the boat. Bill began constructing the travois, which would enable him to do his share of the work.

When he'd been sitting in the cabin the day before, Bill had cut holes in the hide, which he now held. These holes were an inch apart and ran the full length of the leatherlike material. They extended up both opposite sides of the hide, which was just big enough to hold one quarter of the meat. He cut two poles, and then to these poles he began to lash the piece of hide. He did this by using the leather strips that he cut the day before. These strips were weaved through the holes, then around the poles, and soon he had a device that would enable him to drag the meat down the hill. With the hide fastened up a foot from the bottom of the poles, the meat would not drag on the ground. It would be clean upon reaching the river, and because the apparatus could be dragged, Bill knew he would be able to accomplish the feat. He would not follow the path taken by Tom, but go along the game trial, thereby avoiding many fallen logs or growth that would hinder his progress.

Bill was not completely convinced that his plan was foolproof. He knew, however, that something had to work; if not this, then he'd have to try something else. Eventually, in time and with patience, he would surely devise a tool that would enable him to pack meat. Hunting was a large part of his life, and somehow he would overcome the problem, if not this year, then surely before next year's hunt.

As events began unfolding, however, Bill realized that his fears had been unfounded. Had he known earlier that this apparatus would work so well, he'd certainly have used it earlier.

The game trail that led to the river was, of course, a longer walk than the path that Tom had taken. With no deadfall to hinder his advance, however, Bill had little trouble moving a quarter at a time toward the canoe.

Within a few hours, the men stood on the riverbank, resting. Bill waited while Tom's breathing returned to normal. When he was sure that Tom had taken plenty of time to swallow the crow, he fought off the urge to say, "I told you so." Instead, he said, "It's getting late, Tom. Let's get organized here and head for home."

Once the transported meat was in the canoe, the men started down the river toward home. Tom had learned a lesson that day; never again would he doubt the ability of his friend. He knew now that if Bill should want to do something, anything badly enough, he would find a way to accomplish it.

At home, the men peppered the meat, wrapped it in cloth, and then hung it in the shade behind the main cabin. Chico came down from the ledge and sat under the meat pole as he'd done before. He would stay there night and day until the meat was ready to be cut up and canned or dried, whichever the case may be. Bill knew that if any animal should venture near Chico's position, he'd fight to protect this prize. He now regarded the protection of the meat as his responsibility.

CHAPTER 32

B OB CAME UP from the lake and called to Bill. "The fish are in the river. There are an awful lot of them this year. That river down there is alive."

"Okay, Pop, I guess I know what has to be done now."

Each year the kings come out of the Bering Sea. They follow the Yukon River to its source, entering its many tributaries along the way. They had now reached Big Salmon Lake and completed what the men believed to be the longest salmon run in the world. To reach here, the fish must travel over two thousand miles of water. Even though they have such a long trip, the fish remain in good shape when compared to other species in other waters.

The path taken by the kings takes them through deep water and few rapids; therefore, their journey does little damage to the bodies of these monarchs of the north.

They were here once again, and the residents of the lake had the opportunity to catch and preserve them once more.

The following day was spent gaffing enough of the salmon to provide themselves and the dogs with enough fish to maintain a well-rounded diet for the year to follow. When the men felt they'd taken enough of the salmon to accomplish that purpose, they returned home. In so doing, the fish were left to carry on with their age-old ritual. They would now, upon reaching their spawning grounds, lay their eggs. The males would fertilize these eggs, and then male and female, their purpose in life complete, would die. The cycle would repeat itself once the eggs hatched.

After reaching home, the men began cleaning their catch. This took them well into the night. When they finished cleaning, Tom climbed the tree up to the cache. He opened the door and then began pulling the buckets of fish up with a rope; they would be stored here until morning.

This was one of the best times of the year in the valley. It was a time for hard work, yes, but it also signified a renewal of a way of life. This was harvest time, if you like, for those who live in the wild. This year, everything was good so far. The winter's meat was hanging behind the cabin, and there was plenty of salmon for another year. It had been a good spring, and Donna had recently preserved many berries. The mushrooms too were plentiful; they'd been able to pick many of those close to the cabin. All things considered, this year had been exceptional.

Though this was a time for joy, it was also a time to be very careful. The salmon were in the river, everyone knew that, and so did the bears. Bears had a ritual too. For as long as the salmon had been coming to this river, so too came the bears. They gathered along the river, feeding on the fish. In coming to and from the water, they passed daily, dangerously close to the cabins. It was a fact well-known and heeded by all who lived here.

Sometime during the night, a commotion was heard outside the cabins. Bill grabbed a rifle and went outside cautiously to see what the ruckus was all about. When he opened the door, the moon was shining, illuminating the whole yard. He then heard Chico's growls behind the cabin and proceeded in that direction. When he came around the corner of the cabin, the bear swung a massive paw and struck Chico full on the head. The dog yelped and went down. Unaware or uncaring as to Bill's presence, the bear went over to the meat pole, grabbed a quarter of moose meat with his mouth, and pulled it down. In doing so, he broke the cross pole, which spanned two trees, causing the rest to fall as well. The bear then started for the trees. Bill stood in awe for a moment, not believing the size of this monster. As Chico lay there, in a pool of blood, Bill raised his rifle and emptied the magazine before the bear finally fell to the ground.

Chico lay for many days not moving and not eating. As the days wore on, he became thinner. He tried to rally, and his heart held on to the life he'd come to love so much. Bill spent many hours caring for his dog and trying what he could to make things easier for him. Chico was now blind in one eye. Though the bleeding had stopped days ago, his head from jaw to the base of his ear was one large hairless sore. Bill sat over him early one morning, remembering, knowing that his friend was nearing the end of his race. He reached down to touch Chico's large rib cage to let him know that he was there and that he cared. Chico whined, then quivered and passed away. Bill would go on now without the friend that meant so much to him. Never would he forget the devotion and blind love that was Chico.

Bill buried his dog up above the ledge that overlooked the cabins. Here the rock stopped and the dirt began; he buried Chico deep so nothing would disturb him as he slept. Bill sat on the ledge and looked down at his mother's grave. *Chico would like it this way*, he thought. From here he could see everything that mattered to him in the world. From here, he could watch over the cabin and the dogs. He could see far enough down the lake to know when an intruder should happen to stray into his domain.

"I'll miss you, boy. God knows how I'll miss you."

CHAPTER 33

I N THE WEEKS that followed, life became less hectic. The preserving was completed, the woodpile had grown, and the men began concentrating once again on finishing the lodge. Very little work remained to be done. While Bill and Tom had been busy preparing for winter, Bob had kept working on the structure. He now had the petitions built and in place. Only the stairs, which would lead to the second floor, were yet to be completed. There was much trim work to do, but they had the whole winter to complete that.

One morning Bill and Donna were eating breakfast when Donna got up from the table and went out to the porch. Bill followed, wondering if she had become ill. He walked up beside her and saw that she was sick to her stomach. He became worried then and asked her if she wanted to go into Whitehorse.

"No, I'll be all right, Bill. It comes and goes."

"Comes and goes! How long have you been like this?"

"About two months now, I suppose."

"Two months, and you're sure it's not serious?"

"Oh, it's serious all right."

"Donna, what kind of game are you playing with me? If it's serious and has been going on for two months, then I would like to know what it is. If you know, tell me, and if you don't, let's go to town."

"You are going to be a father, Bill. You've been so busy that I haven't had a chance to tell you about it. Sometime near the end of March, we will hopefully become parents."

Bill never went back inside right then; he did eventually, but first he had to tell his father. He rounded up Tom too and invited them over for breakfast. He sat there eating what was left of his now-cold meal. Bill went on and on about the things he planned to do with his child. Bob sat and remembered what it had been like for him when he eagerly awaited the arrival of Bill. Tom too thought to himself as Bill rambled on. He thought of Wendy and how serious his feelings had become for her. Soon he would ask her to become part of his life. He wondered if she could become part of the life that he loved so very much. When the conversation wound down, it was well into the morning. Bob and Tom went out and began to work on the lodge. Bill sat with Donna and asked her many questions about her condition. Not having any need for nor interest in information pertaining to pregnancy until now, there were many things about it that Bill did not understand. He wanted to know now, and Donna patiently explained her condition to him.

The men agreed later that Donna should go into town and have a complete checkup. Donna agreed.

Bill contacted Harvey on the radio that afternoon, and the next morning, he and Donna flew into Whitehorse. From there they flew to Vancouver to see Donna's parents, who were almost as excited about the news as Bill had been. While Donna was undergoing tests the following morning, Bill went downtown and made arrangements to advertise the services of a fishing camp. Big Salmon Tours would begin accepting bookings for fishing trips immediately. These tours would consist of a six-day trip for two parties of two individuals. Adults as well as children were welcome. The tours would begin June 15 and extend through September 15. The ads were to be listed in two well-known outdoor-sports magazines. A Whitehorse address was given, and applicants could write for further information.

They spent a week with Donna's folks and then returned to the lake.

Once again the men began to work on the lodge. The building had demanded much of their time over the previous year, but now it would soon be finished.

They were sitting in the lodge late one morning. Work had stopped temporarily while they sat and drank their coffee. Donna had come from her cabin with more coffee and sat beside her husband. She had begun to show now, and as the days wore on, she took to walking in an effort to escape her discomfort. Now, however, she was sitting with the men, joining in their conversation.

"Bill, have you decided which of us will live here in the lodge?" asked Donna.

"Yes, I have had some ideas about that. To start with, I thought it would be nice if Mom and Dad could live here. Now that Pop is alone, I don't know how he'd feel about that," said Bill.

"Son, I don't have any intention of moving from the cabin," said Bob. "I've lived there for a long time now. I wouldn't feel right about leaving it.

In any case, I couldn't put up with the noise in here. Once the people start coming, this place will be a beehive of activity at times. I've come to enjoy my privacy, and I need quiet to read and write. I'm looking forward to this new endeavor of ours, but it will be necessary to detach myself from it now and then. I'm afraid my patience is not what it used to be. I'm also looking forward to spending time alone with my first grandchild. My cabin will provide a perfect place for that."

Tom spoke up, "Bill, if your father is not interested in moving in here, and it appears that he isn't, I would like to say something on the subject. Donna will be spending more time in here than any of us. Come spring, there will be a child to look after. I feel the only decision that makes any sense is for the two of you to move in here. There is a well in the kitchen, the root cellar is under the building, and everything necessary is under one roof. In the afternoon, the baby can nap in its own bed where Donna can watch over it. I could move into your cabin."

Bill looked at Donna; she nodded her head and said, "I had pretty much the same idea, Tom. It will make things much easier for me this way. I didn't want to push my point on you guys, but I'm glad you feel the way you do. Thank you!"

Soon the lodge was complete. Bill and Donna moved in two days before Christmas, and by Christmas Eve, their home within the lodge was set up exactly as Donna had hoped. Tom had a cabin of his own too, when the plane touched down on the lake.

Bob looked out the lodge window when he heard the engine coming closer to the dock.

"Who could be here this time of night?"

Unknown to Bob and Bill, there was a housewarming party planned. If Bill would have thought about the strange actions of Tom and Donna during the previous days, he would surely have suspected something. He'd been busy though, and he didn't pay any attention to the odd actions of the pair. Donna had been preparing for days. She had baked bread, cookies, and cakes. Yesterday she made some moose sausage, and this morning she decorated a tree in the lodge. Tom had kept the fire burning after the work in the main building was complete. He built a small sleigh, which could be pulled by one dog. He'd made sure the doors upstairs were kept open. He was positive now that all the rooms were well heated. Tom had brought a large turkey from town after his previous visit. In spite of all these things, Bill had no idea, even yet, that this Christmas would be a time to remember.

Harvey and his wife came in the door first, followed by their two children. Harvey was introducing his family when the children noticed the fireplace and ran off to be near it. As the children watched the fire leaping around the logs, Donna's parents appeared in the doorway. Not expecting to see them here, Donna became very emotional. After warm greetings were exchanged between the three, she introduced her parents to Bob. Donna then looked around the lodge for Tom; she wanted to thank him for the unexpected pleasure he had arranged. She couldn't see him anywhere and decided to thank him later. Then Roger came in with his wife. Donna and Bill shook hands with them, not knowing who they were. Bill's father came over then and introduced them.

"Roger was with Tom the day they found you out at Brown Creek."

"Pleased to meet you, Roger. Tom has told me a great deal about you. I'm glad that we have finally met."

Then somebody said, "Where is Tom?"

"He's out talking to Wendy. They'll be here in a few minutes."

Bob and Roger began to talk, and Donna's father shortly joined them. Dan had never been involved in an experience like this. He'd tried hard to avoid coming, but Elsie had been insistent about it; now, here he was. He couldn't help but marvel at this building, and he wandered off to explore the huge facility.

Tom and Wendy came in then, followed by Tom's parents, and the first of many lodge parties was underway.

The party and Christmas Day was the first time Donna had ever experienced feeding and caring for a number of people. The two-day ordeal she had undergone made her realize that she would not be able to handle the fishing parties by herself. If she was going to enjoy the lodge and the people who were to pass through it, she must have help. She talked it over with Bill, and he agreed.

Tom's parents had agreed to handle the bookings for them. The first booking had come in; the trip was scheduled to begin August 1. They'd need many more to fill the four-month period from June 15 to September 15, but they now had a start. Donna started a scrapbook the day she received the deposit. Little did she know at the time, but this man who arranged that first trip would become near and dear to their hearts.

Tom left for town in January. There was little or nothing to do on the lake for him. He decided to spend the rest of the winter with his parents. Bill went in with him to buy a snowmobile. Now that the lodge was complete, he began to build interest once more in the trapline. Chico had been the last of his dog team; now he was gone. By this time, Laika was the mother of many pups. Bill had kept the better of them and sold the others. He knew that they would make a good team, but there had been no time to train them. If he was going to trap, then a snowmobile appeared to be the means to make it possible.

He was content out on the trapline; something about the silence filled him with a respect for this land. Here he felt that the world and all its troubles mattered very little. Here he could be at peace with himself.

Late in March, a baby cried. The noise echoed across the lake, heralding the arrival of the newcomer. Robert William Walker came into the world and made it perfectly obvious that he was not impressed with his new home.

I appeared into this world early in the morning of a beautiful sunny day. The cold days of winter had passed, and spring would soon begin to signal her arrival. The days were becoming longer and longer, and winter's storms were losing their punch.

My father found it hard to go about his business in those first few days of my life. He was very proud of his new son, who seemed so healthy and so very helpless. Proud too he was of my mother who had accomplished this feat and who had insisted that I be born at home. Dad had not been convinced that her idea was a good one, but he had gone along with it. He was happy in the knowledge that it was over and both his wife and child were happy and healthy.

My grandfather had waited patiently for this day to arrive. His days of hard work and cold winter escapades were over now. No longer could he work hard for hours, and the cold seemed to drive itself right into his bones. Working on the lodge had been hard for him. He'd never complained, and his son did not know that many mornings his iron will had got him out of bed. When the lodge began to near completion, he'd been very grateful. Now that it was complete, Grandpa was proud he'd had a part in its construction, but he needed rest.

A child would give him a purpose, someone to spend his time with. This child meant that he could still be helpful to his children. He felt that there would be many days when Dad would be away, Mom would be busy in the lodge, and he would spend time with me. In this way, he felt he could be useful for many years to come, and he was right.

My father spent the bulk of his time then working in preparation for the fishing parties, which began to arrive in June. June 15 was the day the first party arrived. It was on that day too that the final booking for the season was received. Our summer would be filled with strange faces and different personalities behind each one. This fact did not bother my father though; he felt that all people are basically good. In later years, he would say many times that strangers are just friends we haven't met yet. I'll be ever grateful for growing up with that philosophy of his.

Tom returned with the first party of fishermen. He tried to keep his chin up, but Dad noticed that there was something bothering him. Pop was not a prying person, so he didn't press Tom for information. He did hope that Tom would talk about the problem soon though.

When one of the fishermen noticed a problem in Tom's attitude, Dad had to say something. "Tom, can I help you with whatever it is that's bothering you?"

"Is it that obvious, Bill?"

"Yes, I noticed it, almost from the time you got off the plane."

"I'm sorry, Bill. I realize that my timing is bad, but it will take time for me to work this out."

"Do you want to tell me about it, Tom? Maybe I can help."

"Only time will help, Bill. Wendy and I have broken up. I love that girl, Bill, you know that. We've gone our separate ways. I'll hurt for a time, but I know it's for the best. I didn't realize my sorrow was that obvious."

"I wasn't going to say anything about it, Tom. I knew you'd get over it, but Andy noticed, and I had to ask you about it."

"I'll do my best to keep my problems to myself. I suppose, if I keep my mind occupied with other things, it'll help. Thanks for caring, Bill."

As the weeks went by, fishermen came and went. Dad and Tom settled into a routine, which, through repetition, made things much easier for both of them. They were beginning to acquire the skill and knowledge required to do their tasks and work more smoothly.

Tom was in much better spirits when Alice came to the lodge looking for a job. She was a local girl, born and raised in Teslin. Alice had made many trips into this lake in the previous years. Twice she had ridden the river all the way to Carmacks. She loved the valley, and now, after reading the ad in the paper, she hoped she could live here. Almost immediately there became a bond of friendship between my mother and the girl who would help Tom forget his first love.

She was willing to work for small wages during the summer while the fishing was taking place. Dad assured her that in the fall, after operating expenses and overhead costs were calculated, she would receive a bonus based on a percentage of the net profit for the season. During the summer she'd have her own room; her meals would be provided as a condition of employment.

Alice knew that the work would not be easy. She'd have to work seven days a week, from early morning until late evening. The summer would begin in June and continue through the middle of September. The days would be long, but they had always been that way.

Growing up in Teslin had taught her to be tough. Her family had chosen a way of life that differed very little from that here on the lake. She'd have gone on living that life were it not for her love of this valley. When she was a child, her father had brought her here. They'd spent a few days amid the sights and sounds and marveled at the sunrises. She still remembered how the sun sank one evening through a red sky forming the most beautiful sunset she'd ever seen. The following day, the lake had been as clear as glass when she used the water as a mirror to comb her long ebony hair. It was with these memories in mind that Alice made her decision. She would work for these people, who showed so much respect for each other and seemed so happy that she showed such a great respect for the valley that they called home.

During the following months, Alice became very much a part of the family on the lake. Even though we were, of course, not all family, we began to see ourselves as such. Later, as I became older, I realized that others coming to our home also considered us a family unit.

As a youngster, I never realized what a perfect environment I was born into. I cannot ever remember words of anger passing between the mouths of those I love. Often, voices were raised to others who visited our home, to fishermen and children who had little respect for others or for themselves. Even those people were not abused; they just lost the opportunity to return and enjoy our hospitality.

CHAPTER 34

I DON'T KNOW HOW old I was before I began remembering what Grandpa and I did together. I know through the benefit of conversation with my parents that he began reading to me when I was very young. He instilled in me a love for reading; I thank him for that. Through his patience, he was able to give me some of his love for prose and poetry.

The first event that I fully remember about my grandfather is a fishing trip that he and I were on. We took one of the smaller boats out into the lake. Mom had packed us a lunch, and Grandpa planned to spend the afternoon just trolling and enjoying the nice summer day. After being on the water a few hours, I became tired and fell asleep on the bottom of the boat. When I awoke, he was also napping. Before he had gone to sleep, however, he tied some fishing line loosely around my wrist. The other end of this, he tied to his little finger. When I roused from my nap, I pulled on this line in an effort to sit up, and he was also roused. After our naps, we felt fresh, but we weren't ready to go home. Grandpa started the outboard and headed for the point where the river flowed out of the lake. We pulled the boat up to the beach, and we got out. After a hole was dug in the beach, my grandfather began to clean the fish he'd caught during the trip. When that was done and the fish heads and entrails were put into the hole, he washed, and then we began to eat our lunch. We sat there on a log quietly for a few minutes, and then I heard a rustling of leaves just behind me. I looked over to my granddad, and he motioned for me to be quiet. A few seconds passed, then, to my disbelief, three young mink came out of the underbrush and headed in the direction of the hole that held the remains of the fish. They made great haste in carrying pieces of intestines off into the brush where they hid them, then returned to repeat the performance.

They spent quite some time carrying and hiding their treasure. Each time they returned to the fish, my grandfather had crept a bit closer. By the time Grandpa reached the hole, the young mink had become accustomed to him. They did not fear him now as they began trying to carry off the heads of the fish. This was quite a performance in itself because the heads weighed as much or more than the young mink did. They were determined though, and they did reach the willows with a few of them. It was then that Granddad began to cut the heads into pieces, which could be handled much easier by the small animals. As the young mink continued in their endeavor to move all the food to the trees, he began to play a game with them. He'd hold a piece of head out at arm's length, and the animals would come up and take it out of his hand. We began to hold on tighter to the fish and smile as the animals squawked and made it perfectly plain that they were not impressed. During one of these tug-of-war games between man and animal, enough noise was produced to bring the adult minks to the edge of the beach. Grandpa knew that now the game must stop because the adults were beginning to get angry. An adult mink can take a man's finger off with one bite, and he wanted no part of that.

Over the years since then, I've wished many times that somehow we could have captured that experience on film. But film or not, it was an experience that I shall never forget.

From that day on, my granddad and I spent much time together, whether it was walking through the bush or just floating in a boat adrift on the lake, reading from one of the many books he had gathered over the years. I had no way of knowing at the time, of course, but he was the one person who had the biggest influence on the shaping of my character. I know now that a large part of who I am is due mainly to my impression, my love of a man who was a strict disciplinarian but also a caring, gentle, and fair individual.

Shortly after my eighth birthday, my granddad became ill. He lay in bed for days and became ever worse. One evening when my father and I sat at the foot of his bed, his breathing became labored. Dad ran to get Mom, and I was there alone with the man who'd come to mean so much to me. He opened his eyes then and tried to speak. He knew he was dying, and he also knew that I felt he was going to die. My parents returned, and Mom made him as comfortable as possible; there was little else she could do. Grandpa began to talk then; the words came in a hoarse growl.

"Bill, I'd like to talk to you alone for a moment." Mom and I left the room and waited in the kitchen. We listened as my grandfather began to speak once more.

"This life is almost over for me, Bill. I know that. You and I have always been close. We've been much more than just father and son. We've been the best of friends. You have always respected me, and I have returned that respect, I think. You have always been a source of pride to your mother and me. We wanted more children, but that was not to be. We were lucky enough to have only one child, but we've never been sorry for that. We've had a lot of good times together, son. With this in mind, I'd like to give you something to think about. You are at a place now where I was many years ago. You have a fine woman by your side, a son who has been a joy to me. Don't ever let this business thing come between you. If it becomes too demanding, give it up. You can always find another way to make a living. I've said before that few people find true love in this life. Those who do must make sacrifices at times to hold on to it. I hope you'll never have to, but sooner or later, I'm sure that you will. When the time comes, keep your priorities straight and remember the things that are really important and hang on to them at all cost.

"You and Donna are very close, I know that. Your son is getting older now, and he needs more of your time. Take him with you, get to know him, and let him know you. Only through communication and understanding can we grow close to the ones we love. Remember that and practice it. Don't wait until Robby is half grown before you decide to give him your time. If you do, you may find that he has no time for you."

Dad began to weep then as I had been doing for some time. He tried his best to swallow the lump building in his throat.

"Don't cry for me, Bill. There is no need for tears. I have been blessed with a long life and a happy one. I was married young to a woman I've always adored. We had a fine son who, even now, fills me with satisfaction. My body is almost worn out now, but there was a time . . . I'm tired. I'm ready to be with your mother. Soon we will walk together again."

Grandpa slipped into a deep sleep then; Mother and I went back to the lodge and went to bed. Dad lay down on the couch and eventually fell asleep as well.

He woke late the next morning; he'd had a restless night. When sleep finally did come, it lasted until the sun was well up in the morning sky. He awoke with a start and immediately went into his father's bedroom. Bob was not there.

As he was coming out of the cabin, Mother and I came out from the lodge. When we came around the corner, we saw Dad. He was on his knees by his father's side. Grandpa was sitting in a chair on the porch. He sat facing east where he'd watched the sun rise over the lake that he'd always loved. In his left hand, he held a picture of Grandma, and his right hand rested on his favorite book of poems. The book was open and lying

SID BELL

facedown on his lap. Dad began to read the verse that had captured his father's last thoughts. He noticed us standing there as he read the poem aloud. Robert Service, "The Lost Master." How he had loved the works of Service!

Dad buried his father under the rock ledge beside his mother's resting place. When he'd finished saying the appropriate words from the Bible over his dad's body, his mind drifted back to the verse.

He played the game, Lord. He played the game. This was a fitting epitaph for a fine man.

CHAPTER 35

WITH GRANDDAD GONE, I was left pretty much to myself for a few months. Dad was concentrating on qualifying himself to fly Harvey's plane. Harvey wanted to quit flying soon; he was tiring of the business. He'd made good money expediting for mining companies and the government over the last few years. Now he wanted to slow down the pace of his life and spend more time with his family. When he'd made the decision to end his commercial career, he urged my father to obtain a commercial flying license. Once Dad received sufficient flying time, he could take the test and purchase the plane from Harvey. Harvey offered him a much better price for his machine that he had been able to obtain on any other that he'd looked at.

My studies took up most of my morning time, but afternoons just seemed to drag by as the sun began to rise higher in the sky. When the days began getting ever warmer, I became increasingly restless.

I began going for long walks on the pair of snowshoes my father had bought for me. The ice was still in the lake though it had melted outward from shore a few yards. The river was running, free of ice, as I walked along its banks. In places the snow clung to the ground several feet deep. In other places, the ground was bare. It was late in the afternoon as I walked, uncaring and unafraid. As I grew up in the wild, I began to form a dangerous attitude about nature's creatures. I felt that the animals would not harm me if I showed them no malice. Over the years since then, my attitude concerning that opinion has changed, very little, but it has changed. I realize now that behavior patterns differ in animals over the course of the year. Different seasons affect any given situation in different ways. It was on that spring day in May when I learned a valuable lesson about cow moose and their blind devotion to their young. Much like humans, in one respect, moose will fight to the death when defending their calves, if need be.

I had been wandering aimlessly along the riverbank. At times I would stop and watch the grayling in the clear water as their fins broke the surface.

At other times I'd sit on a rock and watch droplets of water as they fell to the creek bed. *The snow would soon be gone*, I thought. Next month the fishermen would be coming back, and this river would be alive with activity for another season.

I was sitting on a large rock watching an eagle soaring in the sky above me when I heard the scrape of rock on rock. I looked up and standing there was a calf moose. It was still wobbly and unsure of its balance. He had surely just recently been born.

If I'd have known then what I know now, I'd have immediately put as much distance between myself and the animal as was possible. However, I did not realize the extent of the danger I was in. Being a child, I was curious to linger and marvel at the beauty that stood before me. I'd been standing quietly for a number of minutes, watching the calf, with a slight breeze blowing at my back. For some reason I still do not understand, the calf bolted and began to run. As it crashed through the bush, I suddenly realized my peril. When I heard water splashing down the river, I began to get scared. I remember then how Grandpa used to talk about hunting these animals. How he had sat in a tree and waited for them to come and go, waiting for a suitable animal that would provide winter meat. I began looking for a tree then, one I could climb. If I could climb high enough, the cow would not be able to reach me. To run would be fatal.

When she came into view, she was on a dead run. Water and small rocks flew as she ran. Straight up the river she came, her ears back and the hair on her hump standing straight up. Never have I seen an animal so mad, and never have I been as happy as I was when I reached a large limb high above the ground. From the limb, I looked down on the cow. I could see the hate in her eyes as she stared up at me. She stood on her back legs, her front legs resting on the tree trunk. Her eyes were bloodred from anger; I could almost guess what she was thinking. I'd been lucky that day, I knew it. I've never forgotten to be extra careful in spring, and I always search for a nearby tree suitable for climbing in case the need should ever arise again.

The cow moose stayed close to the area for hours, and for hours I stayed quietly in the tree as she nursed her calf. When she finally decided to leave, it was almost dark. The sun had dropped over the horizon; enough light remained, however, to watch her as she headed for the thick forest. I remained in the tree until the cow and calf ascended a hill and disappeared over the top into the next valley. Only then did I climb down and head for home.

It was well after dark when I reached the lodge. Mom and Dad had been worrying for hours. They both approached me as I entered. Mom was angry once she realized that no harm had come to me.

"Just a minute, Donna. Before you fly off the handle, we should find out where he's been."

I began to tell the story as best I could, thankful for what Dad had just said. When I'd finished, my father smiled, walked over to me, and gave me a hug. "You're growing up on us, aren't you, son? I've been so busy lately, I've had little time to notice. From now on, we'll have to spend more time together. I've got a lot of things to teach you about the wild. You learned a good lesson today, remember it. I'm only sorry that you had to learn it the hard way. Thank God you had enough sense to climb that tree."

"I didn't get to spend nearly as much time with Grandpa as I'd have liked, Dad, but he did teach me a bit about nature. I am looking forward to learning more from you, but you are so busy."

"Rob, right now I am busy. I've got to spend a lot of time in the air. I have almost got the hours logged that are necessary. A few more weeks and I can test for my license. Once I get that out of the way, we'll spend more time together. I promise you that. This summer you can come with us on overnight fishing trips, and I'd like to take you hunting this fall."

"I'd like that."

"Hang in there for a while, son, and before long we can make up for lost time."

I was feeling pretty good that evening as I ate my supper. I went on and on about the look on the cow's face as she extended herself up the tree, trying to reach me. Even after the excitement of the situation abated and sleep claimed me, I could still see the hate in her eyes. This day will go on living in my memory; someday I will use this experience to help teach children of my own about the wild.

I read somewhere that a person's character and personality traits are formed by the age of eight. I believe this statement to be true. I also believe that beyond this age, a person can round off rough edges and expand on these traits, but basically we are what we will be at a very young age. Therefore, I feel that the first years of a child's life are most important.

It is with this in mind that I give so much credit to my granddad. He has taught me to be happy with the person that I am. I am able now to laugh at life, and even more important, I am able to see humor in the mistakes I make from time to time. This enables me to laugh at myself, and by so doing, the blunder seems to be less important.

On an early morning in June as the sun rose in the sky, I sat on a flat rock beside the river, very close to the location of my previous experience with the cow moose. I quietly thought about how nice it would be to hook one of the large grayling that I could see in the clear water. Where the cold, clear water flowed quickly over the gravel bottom, I could see them as they hovered, almost motionless. They exerted only enough effort to sustain their positions in the fast-moving current at the bottom of the river. They showed very little interest in the spinner that I dangled in front of their noses. For hours I sat there in an effort to attract their attention. I knew that eventually they would feed again, and when they became interested once more in my efforts, I intended to be there. I only hoped I could maintain the patience needed to carry on with the wait.

As time slipped by, my mind began to wander. I could hear my grandfather as he repeated, "Anything worth having is worth waiting for, Rob." He had a lot of sayings like that, which reflected his philosophy on life. Many of these he had passed on to me, and from time to time, I find myself reciting these lines and using the wisdom that they portray.

While sitting there beside the creek, my eyelids began to grow heavy. I lay down then, using the rock for a pillow but still holding my fishing rod out so the spinner remained in the main flow of the stream.

I thought of another one of Grandpa's lines as I drifted off to sleep. "A man doesn't have to be crazy to be a fisherman, but it sure helps."

My sleep lasted only a few minutes, for almost immediately my reel began to scream. I woke with a start and watched as my line went racing across the full width of the river. When it began to come back toward me, I had composed myself a certain amount, but my mind was not working quite right yet. I realized that I must tighten the drag on my reel because this was a big fish, and he was only playing with the tension, set as it was. I did this as the fish came out of the water and danced with his tail on the surface. It became a battle then, the fish doing his best to break the line and free himself. I was just as intent to wear his strength down in an effort to win this prize. He came upstream almost to my location as I quickly reeled in the slack. Then, when almost reaching the rocks, he turned, using the current, his body weight, and his forward thrust in order to break free from the line that held him. While shifting my feet to maintain a better stance from which I could continue the battle, I stepped on a slippery rock and lost my balance. I jumped in an effort to regain my poise, then slipped again and fell headfirst into the fast-flowing water. Down I went, rolling over the rocks, scraping knees and elbows as the current bore me toward deeper water.

I don't know what it was that made me hang on to that fishing rod as I did, but even under the cold water, I could still feel the tug of that fish at the other end of the line. I didn't know or care that deep water was passing under me then; all I was concerned with was winning the battle. Soon, however, the line went slack, and I knew the fish was gone. Then and only then did I become concerned with my situation. When I did realize the seriousness of the circumstances as they were, I knew too that I was indeed in trouble.

A man has little chance when falling into these northern waters, the temperature of which varies little through the seasons. In summer as in winter, they are very cold, and a man unlucky enough to enter into them has but a few minutes. If he should remain in the water, he will be rendered unconscious due to the extreme cold, which will rob his body of the heat essential to life.

My limbs were beginning to tingle from the cold when I saw the tree. The deadfall reached out from the bank and lay over the water. I knew that I could work my way to shore with the help of the tree if only I could grab it and hold on as the current carried me under it. As I approached the point of salvation, I flexed my fingers in an effort to warm them enough to maintain a grip on one of the limbs. The opportunity came, and I tried to reach the shore after grabbing a limb. My hands were too numb though, and the strength needed to accomplish this was gone from my body. Down the stream I went, carried along by a current that was fast becoming my nemesis. The cold had almost sapped my body of its strength when suddenly the water became shallow once more. My body was anchored on a gravel shoal. I mustered up enough strength to pick myself up and walk carefully through the shallow water to the bank. I took my clothes off and lay in the warm rays of the sun until feeling began to creep into my limbs once more.

I stood up then and looked at myself. My knees were raw, and most of my body was sore. My skin was a pale shade of blue caused by the cold; it was hard to tell how badly bruised I'd become.

I thought then how Grandpa would have laughed at the sight of me. Standing there on the bank, naked as a jaybird, I began to laugh.

"Granddad, when you were a kid, were you as foolish as I am?"

I could almost hear him answer, "Yes, and the lessons came just as hard."

Before long, I felt terrific once more, and eventually I mustered up enough courage to pull on my cold wet clothes. After jumping up and down in an effort to become accustomed to the dampness of these, I headed for home. Today I'd be humble; the fish had won, and I had almost lost. I'd been lucky once more. Once again I'd received a cheap lesson, a lesson that would not be taken lightly.

SID BELL

CHAPTER 36

D URING THAT SUMMER, I came to know and love one of the regular visitors who returned to this valley year after year. Jim Dahl was the first man who was ever to book a fishing trip with us. He came back each year in either July or August and was interested not only in fishing but also in shooting the fish and as many of the animals as he could see. He came with his cameras and his lenses in an effort to capture on film the beauty that abounded here. Jim had visited several times previous to that summer, but I hadn't paid much attention to his coming and going.

My father had always felt that a man was only as good as his word. Dad's word was his bond, and if he made a promise, he will do his level best to keep that promise. That summer, I learned many things with my dad and many things about him. I began to appreciate the fact that he very seldom said, "I will do it." Rather, he most often said, "I will try to do it." When he did make a promise, the commitment assured me, as well as all others who knew him, that he would indeed do his best to carry it out.

So it was that summer. He had promised to spend more time with me earlier, and he most definitely did that.

The fishing season was well on its way when Jim arrived during my eighth year. My father, true to his word, had by this time made me a part of the overnight campouts and the daily routines on the river. I'd become an important part, I thought, of the fun and the work involved, which made our way of life a success.

It was during one of these camping trips that my father began to speak of his love for Jim. Previously, I was too young, I suppose, to inquire as to the origin of the high esteem that my parents afforded him.

I was a little older by this time, however, and beginning to take a keener interest in family friends.

As it turned out, Jim was the pastor who married my parents.

There had been an open house at the home of my grandparents in Vancouver following the church service. Jim, being a friend of the family as well as the pastor, was of course invited.

Having been previously asked to deliver a message to the bride and groom, he arrived with a number of pages of rough notes.

When called upon, he stood up and began to speak. "Friends, I have known the bride since she was born, and I met her parents long before that. Of course, then, I have watched her grow through the years, both physically and spiritually.

"Today, the two of you have made one of the most important decisions which this life has to offer. From here you will grow together or drift apart depending, of course, on yourselves. Although I have a good deal of confidence in this union, I would like to offer some words of caution, which you might like to think about.

"A number of years ago, a young man asked me a question. He said, 'Pastor, what is the trick to having a good marriage?'

"Now I didn't care for the idea of using the word *trick* as a descriptive of marriage, and I told him so.

"At the time, the word represented a shady sleight of hand, which makes a situation appear to be true whereas in reality, it isn't true at all.

"Through the years, however, I have thought about this, and I have changed my mind. I'll now endeavor to explain the reason behind this change of heart.

"When we choose a partner and marry, we cease to be a unit. Consequently, we are no longer two but one flesh. Let no man take marriage lightly. 'Let marriage be held in honor among all' (Hebrews 13:4). I say to you, those who have a haphazard approach to life will also have the same approach to wedlock. Keep in mind that the efforts you are willing to exert toward your union will directly reflect and parallel the satisfaction that you receive from it.

"People who love one another enough to marry, quite obviously, not only love but also trust and respect their partner. However, I must say this, the marriage must extend beyond the wedding day, and so too must love, trust, and respect.

"To cultivate and maintain love through the years, we undoubtedly need to nurture interest and intelligence. Have enough interest in your partner to support them in whatever their interests are even if they don't exactly parallel your own. Give a little here and take a little there, I believe to be a good rule to follow.

"I would like to caution you, however, too much give and not enough take can, over a period of time, be disastrous. The reverse can also be true.

"With this in mind, then, we must consider the intelligence aspect, which I mentioned previously. Adopt an attitude toward your lives together, which will enable you to stand firm when you know you're right, and that will allow you to give a bit when you feel that you may not be right. If you can do this, I am sure that the rest will work out for you. Always remember, God holds the husband responsible in marriage.

"Remember too that a problem, any problem, will seem much smaller if you talk it over. Never go to sleep harboring a grudge. Communication between couples cannot be overemphasized. Talk things over. Solve small problems before they become large ones.

"Now, because the question was asked of me, I have to mention one more thing, and then I'll sit down. I don't want to imply that I feel a marriage, to be happy, must produce children. I'll repeat, because the question was asked of *me*, I feel that children are the component which ties all the other ingredients together. I sincerely hope that you two feel the same way.

"In summary then, I would like to offer you a picture of the things which I have touched on to nurture and maintain love. What must we show one another? *Trust, respect, intelligence, communication, and kids.*

"I always like to think of the word *trick* when I think of a good marriage and of the five essential props which will make it a success."

Mom and Dad took a copy of Jim's notes that day and still have them tucked away. They bring the notes out of the trunk from time to time and review them. Quietly they thank the man who, years ago, gave his blessing to a couple of kids whose whole lives lay ahead of them.

My father and I met Jim in Whitehorse the day he arrived to begin his visit.

We flew in early that morning to pick up the supplies we'd need for the week to follow. By the time Jim arrived at the airport, we had finished our shopping and were ready to leave for home.

Financially, events had gone very well over the years for those involved in our business. Some years ago, Dad had decided to schedule a week off somewhere close to the middle of the fishing season. During that week, we were by ourselves on the lake, and we could unwind and do what we wanted to do. Two years before this visit of Jim's, the week off was planned to coincide with his arrival. He had become a loved one. It only seemed right that he was involved and a part of our leisure time together.

As we watched Jim walk from the airplane into the air terminal, I began to think how much older he looked from the previous year. That idea was put aside though when he came inside. Though his hair was white and he'd appeared to move slowly as he approached the building, he broke into a run upon seeing my father. As they hugged each other and said their hellos, Jim lifted Dad bodily off the ground. I realized then that this man possessed great strength because my father was not a small man. Once the jubilation began to ebb, Jim glanced my way.

"This must be Robert. He's going to be a big one, Bill."

We shook hands then and talked as we waited for his luggage.

When we reached home, the others warmly welcomed the man who they'd come to have so much respect for. After a royal meal was eaten, we went into the lodge. Jim and I sat in front of the fireplace as he explained the new photography equipment he'd purchased for his trip.

He asked if I'd be interested in coming with him the following day. After I assured him that I was, we began to talk about his previous visits to this valley. Many of his memories were lost to me, but I did recall a few of them.

After breakfast the following day, Jim loaded his gear into the canoe. "Can you run this thing, Rob?"

"Oh yes, I've been running them since spring."

"If I can get you to handle the controls, I'd appreciate it. I'd like to keep my hands free for taking pictures if I can."

"Okay, Jim, I'll do that."

We headed out across the lake when the sun was still low in the sky. There was a large bay at the southeast end of this lake, and this was the area Jim wanted to explore.

As we entered into the mouth of the bay, Jim turned his head and faced me.

"You'd better cut the throttle a bit, Rob. We are coming to some shallow water."

No sooner had he said that than the water indeed did become very shallow. We had to be careful as we picked a channel to follow. Jim lifted his gaze from the water ahead for a moment and pointed toward a narrow strip of land that jutted out into the water. As I started toward the peninsula, I noticed that the bottom of the lake was becoming a mass of weeds. I began to get concerned about the fact that these may begin to wind themselves around the prop when the water became deep once more. On we went toward land, and the closer we got, the deeper the water became.

We tied the canoe to a tree upon reaching the shore. I wasn't sure what Jim was up to, but I felt it would have something to do with taking pictures.

Beyond our position, on the far side of the bay—or what remained of the bay—a pair of Canada geese were swimming. They paid little attention to us until we began to gather logs and limbs, which lay in the area. Once we started carrying these to a point of land extending into the lake, the geese became curiously concerned. They swam to the far shore with their young and stayed while we continued with our construction.

With the wood, Jim began to fashion a small hut of sorts. He used the bigger wood for uprights, and to these he tied the small limbs. Tying the sticks together provided the stability needed to ensure that a wind would not ruin his efforts. Once he'd placed enough sticks together, he was sure that his creation would stand up to the weather; he covered the hut with a tarp. The tarp had been sewn together with just this use in mind. At the bottom, it had a large hole, which was to be used as a door. On the opposite side of the door, there was a small hole, which the camera lens would project out of. This hole was approximately halfway up the tarp so the camera could sit atop a tripod and operate from a stable position. After the camera was set up inside to enable Jim to place the tarp in exactly the right position, the tarp was tied in place. Then the camera was removed, and we left the location.

We returned to the shallow shoal, and just beyond it, the water became deep again. When the ledge plunged to the depths of the lake, we began to fish. Jim suggested that I keep the boat close to the shallow water but far enough away to allow our lures to sink deep.

As we slowly trolled along the edge of the shelf, we began to talk.

"Jim, I want to thank you for bringing me along today. I appreciate this. I've learned a number of things from you today about taking pictures. I've learned some things about you too. Even though I am only eight years old, you have shown me a lot of respect today. You've asked for my opinions even though you must realize that my experience is limited."

"Rob, I've always tried to treat people with the same respect they show me. As far as being only eight years old, age doesn't have anything to do with courtesy. You are expected to show respect to your elders, I know that. By the same token, should your elders not be expected to show you the same consideration? From the time I was a child myself, I've felt that children are much like adults. They are smaller, yes, but we all need love, respect, and understanding. To acquire and retain these things, we communicate with one another. You may not realize it yet, but you are very fortunate to be growing up in this type of environment. When I come here, I witness more love and happiness in one week than I see in the whole year that I spend away from you people. I just wish that somehow you could understand how fortunate you really are."

I didn't realize it then, but up until that day, there was a void in my life. On the day my grandfather passed away, he took with him the intelligence and the wisdom that I had come to rely on so very much. Since then, my relationship with my father improved a great deal, but there was still something missing. After Jim said those things, I realized why the others loved him as they do. I will always remember those words, and I will go on cherishing his friendship.

On the morning of the fourth day, which followed the construction of the blind, we returned. Sunup found us concealed inside the hutlike hiding place that Jim had erected. The geese had become accustomed to the tarp-covered structure and treated it as any other part of the landscape. I was awed by the ordeal, not being able to believe how close the geese came. We sat for hours as Jim took roll after roll of film. Often I looked up from my sitting position and chuckled when I saw his face gleaming brightly with satisfaction. When the film he'd brought along was all exposed, he began to make low noises. The geese, hearing these, began to swim away. As the noises became louder, they swam farther. Once Jim was satisfied that the birds were far enough away, we crawled out of the blind and removed the canvas from the structure. When we were back in the boat, which we'd hidden under a deadfall, we started for the ledge and began fishing once more.

As we talked and ate our lunch, I began to realize that Jim was the first person since Grandpa passed on whom I could really communicate with. He was passing me a sandwich when his rod began to bend. The action caught him by surprise, and he almost lost the rod. However, he rallied quickly, and the fight was on. I reeled in my own lure and stood ready with the net. I could see from the bend in the large rod and the heavy line, stretched tight as a fiddle string, that it was no ordinary fish on the end of the line. I then reached over and turned the outboard off for fear that during the fight, the prop may sever the line. Never have I witnessed such a pull from any previous catch. I was almost as determined to see this denizen of the deep landed as was Jim. The line suddenly went slack, and he quickly began reeling in the loose line. The fish broke the surface of the water then plunged deep once more. *My god!* I thought. *He's huge.* Down he went as the reel screamed! I looked at Jim as he sat there thinking of nothing except the present task. He tightened the reel drag, and the line went slack once more. Up and down the monster went; in and out went the line. Jim began to tire, but so did the fish. The combination of heavy steel line and the increasing drag of the reel eventually wore down the fish's strength, and he finally gave up the fight. Jim began reeling the monster in; he came slowly but surely from the depths. I stood there in anticipation, half expecting the fish to begin the fight anew upon nearing the surface. The fight had left him, however; when his body broke the top of the water, he was dead. I laid the net down; it was not near big enough to land him. Jim handed me the rod and used both hands to lift the fish into the boat. We headed for home.

After reaching the lodge, we weighed Jim's prize. We could hardly believe the scales, but they read thirty-four pounds and thirteen ounces. Jim looked at me then and said, "It would be a shame to cut this guy up, Rob. How do you feel about getting him mounted? I think he'd look great hanging above the fireplace."

I agreed.

We spent the balance of the day sitting, talking about the fish, and going over Jim's plans for the days to follow. He wanted to leave the valley for a few days and take some pictures in areas he hadn't explored yet. We studied maps he'd purchased, which depicted these areas very well.

The following morning, Dad, Jim, and I lifted off the lake and flew in a northeast direction. I held the map on my knee and tried to pick out landmarks as we left our home behind us. We crossed over a ridge and flew over another valley. According to the map, this was surely the valley of the Rose River. We followed the Rose for miles then banked east upon reaching the Lappi Lake. We now followed yet another valley as we approached the snowcapped peaks of a mountain range. We flew above this low land between the large foothills until it merged with another. When the two valleys came together, Jim pointed out a small lake.

"Can you land there, Bill?"

"It looks awfully small, Jim, but we'll go down and have a look."

Not only was the lake small, but also much of it was very shallow. Dad decided he could touch down though, and we landed on Seagull Lake. Why it was called Seagull Lake, none of us could understand, but it was, and we were here.

Once we'd removed our gear from the plane, it was moored a short distance from shore. We'd begun setting up camp when we heard a small animal squeaking as if it were in distress. Jim grabbed his camera as we turned our heads to see a gopher with a mink at its throat. A few seconds was all it took; the gopher was dead. Already Jim's face lit up; he had been in the right place at the right time and had captured the event on film. Nature once more had proven that some must die so others may live.

After camp was made, we had lunch. While the men cleaned up and washed the dishes, they suggested I go down to the creek and catch a fish. I stood on the creek bank and marveled at the number of small trout, which swam up and down the stream, going to and coming from the lake. It was not long until I tired of catching them one at a time, and I began to hatch a plan. There was a shallow pool just below a small rapid. In this rapid above the pool, I built a dam out of rocks. The spaces between the rocks were large enough to allow the water to pass through, but not large enough to allow the fish passage. I waited then until the water became clear once more and the fish began coming into the pool. I'd built the rock dam high enough to prevent them from jumping over it. When the pool began to fill up with these fish, I felt my plan was working. I then went downstream and constructed much the same type of dam, which would block their escape that way as well. I stood there, soaking wet and very proud of myself as my father and Jim came out of the trees. I started into the stream, intent on scooping as many of the fish as possible out of the water and onto the rocks. I didn't even notice the men coming until Dad hollered at me.

"What are you doing there, Rob?"

I was in trouble! When I was hatching the plan, I knew that my father would not approve, but I had continued nevertheless.

"I figured out a way to catch a bunch of fish, Dad."

"What do you plan to do with them?"

"We can eat them."

"Can we? It may be a couple of days before we return home. By then they'll be no good. You've got half a dozen fish lying there now. That's more than enough to last until tomorrow. If we want more then, you can come down and catch some more."

"I never thought about that."

"Well, that's fine, Rob, but don't do it again, okay?"

"If you don't mind, Bill, I'd like to take some pictures of this before Rob tears these dams apart. It seems a shame that he went through all this work for nothing."

"Okay, Jim, go ahead."

"Rob, kneel down over there by the dam, make believe you are still building it."

Jim took a few pictures of me, and then he took pictures of the pool, which was full of fish. Even I had not realized how many had been trapped.

"Bill, Rob, how would you feel about being in a movie? I am toying with the idea of making a feature-length movie from the pictures I've shot here over the years. If you agree to be part of it, I'd like to start working on it this winter. Purely promotional stuff. It pays to advertise."

"Do you have all the material you need, Jim?"

"Almost. I'd like to get some footage of some caribou if I can, but other than that, I have more than enough."

"Well, I don't know how Rob feels about it, but if I won't have to leave home for any reason, I don't mind."

"Rob, how do you feel about it?"

"Go for it. I think it might be neat."

That evening we sat around the campfire. I began to realize, while sitting in the firelight, that I was beginning to build the friendship with my father that I had long wanted. Today had been a good one; Dad had not agreed with my plan to catch so many fish at one time, but he did congratulate me for coming up with a dandy idea. He even said that we may be able to use it sometime in the fall when catching many fish would be imperative to our way of life. He mentioned too that we must respect nature and take no more from her than was absolutely necessary.

I went to bed early that night; it had been a busy day, and I was beat. I woke during the night, and Dad was lying beside me in the tent. Where was Jim though? I looked around the tent, but I couldn't see him. When I walked outside the tent to relieve my bladder, I saw him. He was lying beside the campfire on the ground, his head resting on a rock. I went inside the tent then and picked up the extra blanket that was atop my sleeping bag, returned to the campfire, and spread the blanket over Jim. He never moved, just grunted, and went on sleeping.

I woke to the smell of pancakes and bacon, came out of the tent, and saw Dad and Jim quietly talking. Dad took a small piece of bacon from the pan and handed it to me along with a towel.

"That should hold you until you can get washed up," he said.

I walked down to the creek, got down on my knees, and splashed some water over my face. My whole body shivered from the cold mountain water;

however, it did snap me to attention. I was wide awake when I returned to the campfire. Hungry as a bear, I sat down to a delicious breakfast.

Some time that morning, while I was busy fishing, two men on horseback arrived at camp. They had been up in the mountains hunting sheep. One of the men was a guide, the other a hunter who had returned to the lake to wait for a floatplane that would fly him out to Whitehorse. We came to know these two men quite well during the afternoon. When the plane touched down the hunter climbed aboard and flew off. After he left, we sat at the campfire and talked with the guide, whose name was Lyle. Before he got back on his horse, he offered us some sheep meat. I had never had the opportunity to eat sheep meat before that day; after trying it, and even now, I consider the taste of mountain sheep to be rivaled by no meat I have ever eaten.

The following day, we broke camp and flew southward over a mountain. As we cleared the mountaintop, we looked down at Sheep Creek. The valley looked beautiful. Near the base of the mountains, we could see many patches of snow. It remained cool all the summer through up here. High up in the alpine was the most likely spot to find caribou during the summer months. Here they were able to escape from the flies, and here they lay on these patches of snow to keep cool.

We flew over the area for some time, but we never did see any caribou that day. After flying the length of the valley a few times without success, we left for home.

When we approached the dock, we saw Laika standing there waiting for our arrival. Upon leaving the plane, my father got down on one knee and made a fuss over her. When we entered the house, Mom commented.

"Do you realize, Bill, that's the first time since Chico passed on that you've made any attempt to be friendly toward any of the dogs?"

"Yes, I suppose it is. I hadn't really thought about it, Donna. I guess I haven't been very fair to Laika, have I? It has taken me a long time, hasn't it? It's strange how Laika keeps going on and on. She was about two when we were married, then it was about two more years, I think, until Chico was killed. It's been almost nine years since then. She has to be awfully close to thirteen years old. That's a ripe old age for a dog."

"Yes, she's been a good animal too. Rob spent a lot of good times with her when he was younger. Your father loved that dog a great deal. It's too bad that all of us must get old."

"Donna, I'm going to go to town tomorrow. Jim says he has to leave, and while I'm in there, I'd like to look for a lead dog. I'm going to teach

Rob about trapping this winter, and I'm going to do it right. We have enough good dogs for a team, but they are not experienced. I need a good lead dog to help me give them the training they need."

Before Jim left the following morning, he gave me a camera. I had become quite enthusiastic with the art of photography. I now had the means to continue my interest in a newfound hobby. Along with the camera, he provided me with a telescopic lens and some filters.

"Rob, if you get a chance to shoot some pictures of caribou, I would like to have my choice of the prints. If you can agree to that, then please accept these as a gift."

He said his good-byes and promised to return the following year. We shook hands, and he and Dad climbed into the plane and flew off.

CHAPTER 37

THE NEXT AFTERNOON, Dad returned with a male husky. He was a powerful-looking large beast with cunning eyes and lash marks across his back. He had surely been whipped a good deal in previous years, but the cuts were well healed now. The beating had not affected his attitude in any noticeable manner, for he carried himself well and showed fear of nothing or no one. Dad felt that Chinook was part Siberian and part God-knows-what. He was not colored like a Siberian, but he carried himself as such. His legs were dark gray, and halfway up his sides, the gray slowly turned to black. The hair on his massive chest showed lines that had implanted themselves there from hours in harness. The women took an immediate dislike to Chinook. They never said so in words, but it became obvious that neither Mom nor Alice had any love for the animal.

Tom and my father, however, did like the dog, admiring him a great deal for his obvious strength and experience. Chinook knew that the men respected him, and he returned the favor many times. He surely had known mean men in his life, but he must also have witnessed tenderness. I became good friends with Chinook, and in time, we became inseparable. During the second day following Chinook's arrival, I learned a valuable lesson concerning this dog.

The first week of his stay with us, he was tied to Dad's machine shop. There was no problem with this because he was obviously used to being tied. However, he had also received many beatings during his life; the scars were proof of that. I was walking around the yard picking up sticks in an effort to tidy things up. When I came around the corner of the shop and into Chinook's sight, I stooped down and picked up a stick. Chinook went wild; if his chain had been longer, I am sure I'd have lost the use of my arm for a few days. The surprise of the situation made me drop the stick, and he immediately settled down. I talked to him for a while, and then when I was sure the danger had passed, I walked over to the dog and rubbed his neck. I never made that mistake again, and I told the others about it so they would be careful.

A week passed before Dad felt he could release the animal. He was sure then that Chinook would not run off. He took a chance, and the dog proved him right.

Chinook had learned his lessons well over the years. To be a good leader, one must also be a loner. He did not pay much attention to the other dogs; he kept pretty much to himself. They realized that he was not to be taken lightly. Some accepted this knowledge from the start while others learned it the hard way, painfully. They did learn it though, and Chinook made sure they remembered.

In the evenings, after coming off the lake, Tom and Dad set about building a wagon. When the wagon was completed, they made a harness out of moose hide.

Eventually the needed equipment was completed, and Dad started training his team. Some of the dogs were little more than pups when the work began. They soon realized that there was to be more to their lives that just lying around and getting fat. The mature dogs were worked harder than the young ones, of course, but they all learned.

Soon they began to take pride in themselves, and the good ones among them began to excel over the others. One by one the culls among them were ejected. Of these, a few were too young; they'd be allowed to mature. The others were taken to town and sold. Muscle hardened to the task, and sinew strengthened as the wagon was pulled up and down the beach. Each evening the load was increased, and soon the trip was lengthened. I watched as my father and Tom trained the dogs. I watched and I learned. Tom ran behind the sled, through the sand until his legs became too sore to go on anymore. Dad would rest his artificial leg on the sleigh and push with the other.

As the weeks went by, it became a game as much for us as it was for the dogs. By the time the fishing season ended, we were proud of the progress we'd made. The team was almost trail ready, and they jumped in unison at the command. When the snow began to fly, we had nine sled dogs, all of which were among the best available anywhere.

With the departure of the last fishing party came the need to prepare ourselves once again for the long, dark days ahead. Preparation for the winter months no longer took near the time that it once did. With the fishing parties came the necessity to buy many store-bought goods. Law prevented us from feeding our clients the natural foods that were so bountiful in the valley. Therefore, we were forced to provide them with groceries purchased over the counter. Whenever the season began, we always had plenty of canned goods in the pantry and frozen products in the deep freeze. With the arrival of our busy summer, the generator would be started and remain working until all the leftover meat and vegetables were used up. It would then be shut down and life would continue as it once did and should.

In spite of the fact that things had become easier for us, we still had a need for a supply of wild meat and fish for the dogs. By the time the season would end, the salmon run would long be over, but somehow we always managed to can or smoke enough of the fish for our needs.

Because our harvest time was so much easier now and partly because of the long, demanding summer, Tom and Alice chose to leave the lake with the last fishing party.

They were long married by the time Dad decided to take me on my first hunting trip. That year they left as they always did. Tom's parents were still living in Whitehorse, and they spent two or three weeks with them. When they decided they'd remained long enough and felt they were becoming a burden to his folks, they left.

Alice's mother was still residing in Teslin. Her husband had passed on a few years earlier, and Belinda lived alone now in a small home on the lake. When they left Whitehorse, they took a bus to Teslin and remained there for some time. When they'd had a chance to wind down and ties were strengthened once more with the people they loved, they would radio my father, who would fly down to pick them up. Each year they were gone for a few months, but otherwise they resided on the lake with us.

During their absence, my father and I would embark on a trip of our own, a jaunt that we both looked forward to. We came to realize a few years ago that this was to be our time together. Once a year we left the lodge behind for a few days and lived in the wilderness together. During these few days, we would become aware of small changes that had occurred within us over the course of the previous year. Being truly alone with one another, we can accept these changes and deal with them. It was a time to know each other anew.

CHAPTER 38

S O IT WAS the day we struck out across the lake. We had planned to run the course of the river from home then upstream as far as Quiet Lake. Maybe we'd be lucky enough to see a moose near the water, maybe not. In any case, I hadn't gone beyond Sandy Lake, and I looked forward to witnessing country I hadn't seen yet.

When we passed the slough that lay between Big Salmon Lake and Sandy Lake, Dad headed for shore. "There's a lick up on the hill, Rob. We'll go up and see if they're using it this year." We pulled the canoe up on shore and started walking up the hill toward the lick. As we proceeded, he told me the story of a previous hunt when Tom and he had shot an animal in this area. We reached the lick, and it was obvious that there had been no moose there for some time.

We returned to the canoe and continued up the river toward the line cabin on Sandy Lake. When we reached the cabin, we went inside and came face-to-face with a porcupine. He huddled in the corner as we planned a way to move him out without hurting him. Dad went outside once more and picked up a long pole. He told me to go out and stand behind the cabin so I'd be out of the way. He then walked over to the corner where the animal was cowering and obviously afraid of being hurt. As Dad began to gently prod the porcupine toward the open door, the animal swung his tail. In doing so, he left some of his quills implanted in the wooden pole. Each time my father encouraged the animal to move farther, the pole would again bear the brunt of his displeasure. After a few minutes, the porcupine reached the door and waddled toward the trees out of harm's way. When he had gone, I entered the cabin, and we sat down and had some lunch.

That done, we started for the canoe once more. It was late afternoon, and the moose would begin to move soon. I sharpened my knife as Dad started the outboard, and we proceeded up the lake toward the river. Upon reaching the river, he planned to follow it up as far as the rapids. The summer had been dry, and the lakes were shallow; therefore, we may have to portage the rapids to reach Quiet Lake. If so, we would hunt near the cabin that evening and continue the following day.

As we started up the river, I looked back at my father. He was watching the bottom of the river as it became even shallower.

"You look ahead and follow the channel, Rob. Watch for the deeper water and point toward it. Between the two of us, we may be able to make it through. If we can get through this slow water and up into the rapids, we'll be okay. I know where the channel is up there, but down here I don't. I've never seen the river this low."

As we slowly moved up the river, I kept my eyes glued to the bottom. I watched the grayling too as they quickly swam off to escape the shadow that approached. The river was alive with them. I took my eyes off the riverbed for a second to watch the fish as they darted about. By the time I realized my mistake, it was too late. The canoe glanced off a large rock, and I was almost thrown into the water. Because of our slow movement, the damage to the canoe was not severe. There was, however, sufficient harm done to force us ashore. As we started for the closest ground, it became apparent that the hole was beginning to widen. I was happy knowing that we had this problem in the river and not a lake. If need be, we'd be able to walk ashore and drag the canoe behind us. This would not be possible in lake water, for we'd surely sink. When we reached shore, the canoe was unloaded and dragged up onto the rocks. We turned it over to see the extent of the damage and to dry the area that must be patched. With a towel, we rubbed it dry then waited for the air to completely dry the damaged area. From the fiberglass patching kit, we cut a patch large enough to cover the hole. Resin and hardener were mixed together, and the patch was saturated and then placed on the canoe. Once we applied sufficient coatings of fiberglass resin to the area, we waited for our work to dry.

While the patch was drying, we went for a short walk. Dad knew of a few game trails in the area, and we proceeded up the riverbank on foot to look at these paths. When we approached Quiet Lake, we noticed prints in the mud. Animals had been crossing the river where it left the lake. The water was shallow at this point and moved slow enough to enable even the young animals with a fordable route.

Dad kneeled and studied the tracks very closely.

"Rob, did you bring your camera with you?"

"Yes, I did. It's in a plastic bag with the gear."

"That's good. We may just get the pictures that Jim wants. Moose have been crossing here, Rob, but early this morning, there was five or six caribou here as well."

"Do you think they'll come back?"

"Not likely, son. Being caribou, they'll be far away from here now, but their being here proves that they are on the move. They were here, that means there'll be others, and we'll be waiting for them.

"Let's go back to the canoe and make ourselves something to eat. It will be a long night, and we won't have a fire to warm ourselves. I'm glad now that we brought our sleeping bags. See that hill across the river, son? That's where we'll sleep tonight. From there we'll watch the river, and we'll see everything that might cross it."

We returned to the canoe and built a small fire. The canoe was moved closer to the heat. Dad felt that the patch had dried nicely, but the heat from the fire would add a little insurance. We ate the meal Dad prepared over the coals and talked.

"Have you ever hunted caribou before, Dad?"

"Yes, I have, Rob, not often and not very successfully, but I have hunted them. Caribou, for some reason, don't hang around this valley for long. Once in a while, I've been lucky enough to see a few of them as they pass through here but not many. They spend the summer high in the mountains in alpine country. Sometime in the fall, they move to their wintering grounds. In doing so, they pass through here, but they don't stay for long. I don't know where they spend the winter, son, but I do know that they go beyond this valley. From what I have been told, caribou travel in herds, but the few times I've seen them, they've been traveling in small groups. Six, sometimes seven, animals have passed through here. I've seen their tracks many times but have rarely witnessed the sight of them. I've only shot one caribou. It was quite a few years ago. I was not much older than you are at the time. My father and I were out moose hunting, and it happened quite by accident.

"We were downriver from home. A squall came up quickly, and we'd taken refuge under a tree. The sky had turned dark, and it began to snow within minutes. The wind blew in gusts and whipped the snow around in circles. We sat under the pine as the wind grew stronger and began to pick the snow off the ground and mix it with that which was falling steadily. Then the wind died, and as quickly as the squall had started, it was over. We both stood up and shook the snow from our clothes. While we stood there not believing what had happened, three caribou stood up. They had been lying not fifty yards from us. They must have come with the wind at their backs and lay down to escape the storm. Dad saw them first, but he let me do the shooting. That was the first and last caribou that I've ever shot."

When we finished eating, the canoe was put into the water once more. We put the fire out and loaded our gear up once more. We no longer had any reason to run the rapids, for it was only a short distance from our vantage point. It was necessary, however, for us to cross the river to begin our walk. We did this with no difficulty, however, and upon reaching the other side, the canoe was hidden in a small inlet and tied to a tree. We took the supplies we'd need plus my camera and began the steep climb to the top of the hill where we'd spend the night.

Between the two of us, we made the decision that I would operate the camera and Dad would look after the rifle. We were lucky enough to enjoy good weather, and it remained rather comfortable temperaturewise until late into the night. Even then, we remained quite comfortable wrapped in our sleeping bags atop the pine bough beds we'd made.

Just as dusk began to settle over the river, we watched three moose come down from the hill on the far side of the stream. They lingered a short while, then drank from the cold stream and carried on, entering the trees below our position. We could have taken one of them home with us, but Dad was so sure we'd see a caribou that he'd lost interest in the moose for now. He let them go, and as darkness fell, he began to have second thoughts about his premonition concerning the caribou. He told me about his feelings and the fact that he may have made a mistake about letting the moose proceed unharmed. By this time, I too had gained the confidence that we would indeed see or hear caribou as they moved across the river. It was a mutual decision to remain in our location through the night. Darkness had fallen, and though there was not enough light for us to shoot an animal, morning would bring a fresh opportunity and allow us to continue our vigil.

Shortly before sunrise, another moose crossed the river from our side. We watched him as he walked up the hill on the far side of the river and disappeared into the pines. We were beginning to get hungry, and our stomachs were grumbling with displeasure when we heard a sort of clicking noise. It came from the far side of the river, and it grew ever louder. I realized that whatever it was, we'd surely get a look at it, for it sounded very close, and it was coming ever closer as the minutes ticked by.

"Rob, come closer and focus your camera. Get yourself set because the time has come. You are going to get some pictures."

When the animals came out of the bush, the sun was shining. We couldn't have ordered better picture-taking conditions. They came surely and steadily out into the clearing that was the riverbank. I sat in disbelief at their beauty. They lingered along the bank and drank as others appeared steadily. When the first to arrive had satisfied their thirst, they moved across the water, making room for the others that came in a steady flow from the trees. All the while I watched them through the camera lens. I hoped that I'd made the proper settings as I watched and clicked. I knew that I may never again witness the beauty of these animals, and it would be nothing short of a tragedy if I'd made a mistake. Film after film was shot, and still they came.

When I ran out of film, their numbers began to abate. It was then that Dad nudged me, and I moved out of the way. He lay down on his stomach, raised his rifle, squeezed the trigger, and a large caribou was ours.

To this day I have not seen any spectacle of nature that has moved me the way these caribou did. I have seen this phenomenon every year since then, in the same place, but that first sighting will remain in my mind. I will remain in awe at the sight of what I believe to be one of nature's most extraordinary yearly events.

As we dressed the animal, I asked my father the questions that had plagued my mind for hours.

"Why do these animals produce a clicking noise when they walk?"

"From what I can understand, Rob, the noise is produced by a tendon in the animal's foot. During the natural movement of the foot while the animal walks, a tendon slips over a bone. It is the coming together of these and through slipping over each other that the sound is produced. When the animals run, this sound becomes even more audible."

"I noticed that all the adults had antlers. Were they all bulls?"

"No, Rob, caribou are the only members of the deer family in which both male and female alike have antlers. They travel together twice a year from their wintering ground to their summer home and back again when spring arrives. They travel in large herds, I expect, because there is safety in numbers. Nobody really understands what triggers the migration, but I'm glad we waited for this. I too have learned much today. I have waited longer than you have for this, and I am every bit as impressed with the spectacle as you are. From now on, we can take one animal each fall. Hunting will be much easier now, I'm glad for that.

"We don't have enough meat here for our needs, Rob, so we'll have to try and get a moose on our way home. Let's go have breakfast and figure out how we can get this animal downriver to the canoe."

After we ate, Dad built a raft and loaded the meat onto it. He then rode with the meat downstream through the rapids to quiet water. When he could, he beached the raft, and we transferred the meat to the canoe. As we left the area and began to drift downriver, I thought once more about the exhibition we had witnessed. We hadn't counted the numbers of animals, but I couldn't help but speculate. I guessed there must have been close to a hundred caribou in the herd.

Evening had come, and as the valley slipped into darkness, we arrived at the Sandy Lake line cabin. We spent the night there in the warmth and comfort that it provided. When morning arrived, we proceeded toward home. Upon leaving the lake, we entered the river once more and continued our journey toward Big Salmon Lake, our home water. The journey from the cabin had been uneventful, but as we left the river once more and approached the lake, Dad turned the motor off. The movement of the river carried us out into the lake. Steadily and quietly, we moved toward the wider, deeper water. It was then that we heard a splash, and we each in our own minds felt certain that an animal had entered the water. When we broke into the clear, we looked down the length of the bay. The morning mist was burned off by the heat of the sun, and the air was clear above the water.

A lone yearling calf had entered the lake earlier and was swimming toward the far side of the bay. He watched us as he swam; Dad started the outboard motor as the calf passed the halfway point and continued toward the shore. Dad handed me the rifle as we continued toward the calf.

"Wait until he reaches the shore, Rob, then aim carefully and squeeze the trigger. Try to shoot him high in the neck. If you can hit the joint, he won't suffer. Moose have a large blade bone in their front shoulder. If you can break that, he will fall. Whatever you do, make sure that he doesn't get back into the water. If he does, he'll die there, and we certainly don't need that."

We came ever closer to the moose as he reached shallow water once more. He stood for a moment and watched our approach, then turned and began to walk toward shore. My father turned the canoe, so I was facing the animal. I would not have to turn my body when I shoot. He turned the motor off once more as we sat and waited for the calf to reach ground. When he did, he turned his head once more to watch us. I squeezed the trigger, and the animal fell. He'd provided me with a perfect neck shot; he died instantly and painlessly, and we were glad for that.

After the moose was dressed and quartered, we loaded the meat into the freighter canoe and left. Upon reaching home, we hung the meat on the meat pole. After Chico had been killed, Dad raised the cross pole much higher than it had been. It spans the two trees much higher now. As the meat hung there, it remained some eight or nine feet above the ground, well out of reach of most bears that may frequent the area. After Chico's death too, the decision was made to start the hunt after the salmon had spawned and their carcasses were carried away by the river's current. This decision greatly reduced the possibility of having bear trouble.

CHAPTER 39

WITH THE WINTER'S meat hanging behind the cabins, we began to concentrate on storing our fishing equipment, which up until then had been left in the water. Motors and gas tanks were taken to the toolshed where they'd remain until spring. The boats were carried up from the lake and placed upside down and away from future winter ice. Soon we would have to pull the airplane out of the water as well, but for now, it would remain afloat. Dad went to town a few days later for some trapping supplies, and when he returned, it was snowing. The nights began to get colder, and we spent more time indoors.

We were cutting and canning the meat when Tom called on the radio. He and Alice were ready to come home again.

"I'll have to spend the rest of the day cutting meat, Tom, but I can pick you up early tomorrow morning. If you need anything from town, you should pick it up today. Once we get back to the lake, we'll be stuck here until the lake freezes over. It's snowing here, and the nights are getting quite chilly, so the plane has to come out of the water."

"That's fine, Bill. We'll look for you in the morning then. How's the tractor running? Have you started it? We'll use it to pull the plane up onto the beach, I suppose."

"No, I haven't tried it, Tom, but I will. If there's any problem, I'll phone you back."

"Okay, I'll be near the phone. I've no place to go."

"Fine, Tom. We'll see you tomorrow then."

"Yes, we're looking forward to that, over and out."

While the idea was still fresh in Dad's mind, he went out and started the tractor. It turned over twice then fired up like a champion. He let the tractor run for a while, then turned it off, and we went into the toolshed. He looked for a tow cable and clevis that we'd need to pull the plane onto the beach. While he was looking for these, I noticed a small sleigh. It stood in the corner under a layer of dust, looking as though it had never been used.

"Dad, where did this sleigh come from?"

"I'd forgotten all about that, Rob. Tom built it before you were born. When we'd finished the lodge, Tom and your mother planned a surprise party and invited our friends. Harvey's kids were small then. Tom built the sleigh for them to use while they were here. They never did use it though. It was the Christmas before you were born, son. Those kids were so fascinated by the fireplace and their gifts, they never went outside. It's been lying there for almost eleven years now, I guess. When we get back from Teslin tomorrow, Tom and I will hook up one of the dogs for you, providing that the snow keeps falling. Help me find a clevis, Rob, and then we'll dig that sleigh out and have a look at it."

The following day, Tom said that I could have the sleigh. In the winters that followed, I spent many hours and many days teaching the younger dogs to pull me around. With the use of that sled, I gained knowledge. I also gained respect for the dogs, respect that I hadn't felt earlier in life. With respect came trust and friendship not only on my part but as I learned more and worked with the animals, they began to see me in a new light as well. I began to communicate with them as only a lover of animals can. When they excelled at their task, I praised them, and I began to feel a pride within myself as well.

Within a month following the first snowfall, ice surrounded the lakeshore. It was strong enough and extended out into the water far enough to allow travel with the dogsled. Temperature dropped, and soon the river too was safe to travel on. Trapping became an important part of my life that season. My father spent many hours teaching me about dos and don'ts of the art that this country was founded on.

As my knowledge grew, I began to realize that the dogs played a large part in this new experience I had undertaken. I learned too that the relationship between a man and his dogs must be one of trust and respect. The lead dog, if he was a good one, could help a great deal in teaching the other animals about discipline. Each dog in his turn would make certain that the animal ahead of him will not let the traces go slack. When he does, if he does, he'll receive a nip on the leg, thereby encouraging him to pull his share of the load, once more.

Because of his previous accident, Dad was no longer able to run behind the sled. His foot and the lower part of one leg were artificial now. The leg had been amputated four inches below the knee, which enabled him to do most of the things he once did, but running was one exception. Running in deep snow was totally impossible for him. He realized this when he decided to return to working the trapline. The added weight of his body, he thought, would be too demanding for a small team, so he decided to maintain a larger one. His team now consisted of nine dogs. He supported the weight of his body on the back of the sled, standing on the artificial leg and pushing with the other one. Between the use of extra dogs and Dad pushing the sleigh along, they traveled for miles and never tired.

When I think back to those times, as I often do, my mind recalls the morning when Pop was sitting in a snowbank as I came from the cabin. As I approached his position, my father stood up and shook the snow from his clothing. Just then the dogs began to fight. The snow flew and mixed itself with the blood and hair that began to dot the immediate area. Dad grabbed a stick and began beating the dogs, trying to part them. With help from Mom and me, the dogs were separated. As we rested, sitting in the snow, I said to my father, "Dad, why do you do it?"

"Why do I do what, son?"

"Why push yourself this way? The money you make from trapping hardly justifies driving yourself the way you do. Every winter, year after year, you fight the snow and these dogs until you become completely exhausted. Each night you fall into bed spent, and every morning, six days a week, you are up and working before daybreak. If you needed the money, I could understand, but you make more than enough to live on during the summer. Why do you do it?"

"If I knew, I could explain it, son. I do know that we have no control over how we feel nor can we understand what drives us.

"Someone once said that all the world is a stage and we each must play our parts. That statement is so true.

"We are not in control. We cannot say from one day to the next what will take place. We must realize that we can only live our lives according to God's predetermined plan.

"I suppose that I am a person in whom the Creator has instilled the need to keep busy. I become restless when I am idle. Working comes much easier to me than sitting. You may not understand now, but you will someday because I have noticed that you are becoming much the same yourself."

I could not understand fully at the time, but I have quietly meditated on those words since. I realize now that any serious-minded person who takes the time to think has to admit that there are many questions that need to be answered. I am thankful that I have received the answers to some of these. Thanks goes largely to my parents for creating a thirst within me, which leads ever closer to the truth.

The remainder of that winter was tough as so many of our winters were. There was no break for ten or eleven weeks. The mercury plunged to sixty below often and didn't climb above minus forty-five for over two months. All of December, January, and part of February were almost unbearable.

Lessons that had been learned in previous years taught my parents the value of being prepared. We therefore had no hardship other than the discomfort that the unbelievably low temperatures caused.

The wild animals were not quite so fortunate. All of them undoubtedly paid a high price, but the moose suffered the most. The deep snow made moving difficult for them.

The weather was so cold, and the winds packed the surface. In order to move at all, the big animals had to break this crust, and that, even for a moose, was tiring. To compensate for this, they gathered in groups and stayed in one area. This action did not only lessen the snow problem, but it also provided a greater protection. There was safety in numbers.

The crust on the snow had become so thick that the wolf pack was able to run along on top. The moose had to move slowly and, because of their greater weight, broke through the crust. Whenever the animals exhausted the food supply available in their chosen alder haven, they were forced to move. When they left the area, which was trampled down due to their constant foraging for fresh growth on the trees, they also left their safety zone.

The wolves knew that eventually the large animals would have to move. Knowing this, they were never far off. When they did move, the wolves would eventually bring one down. The moose that was chosen by the pack was doomed from the start. It was only a matter of time until the wolves, aided by the crusted snow, would tire the big animal, and then nature's course quickly followed.

If this kept up, it seemed quite likely that come spring there'd be no moose left. Circumstances and advantage were clearly on the side of the pack. When the moose's situation seemed impossible, and we were sure that it could get no worse, it did!

The herd, which had already been dealt a crippling blow, began to show signs of tick infestation. In a matter of weeks, their coats became white, and they began to lose their hair.

When the temperature did begin to warm up, we felt that it was too late for the moose population. It had been weeks since we'd seen any of the animals. Those we'd seen then were in such poor shape, we'd wished somehow that we hadn't sighted them at all.

During the summer that followed, we did see a few animals, none younger than two years of age and certainly no old moose. That winter destroyed the calf crop that two seasons had produced.

Nature can wield some stiff blows from time to time. Who are we to question her motives? Yet there is much we do not understand.

A number of years have come and gone since then, and there are at least as many moose in the valley now as there ever were. There have been other times when I have asked the question *why*. I realize, however, that a much wiser mind than mine is needed to answer that question.

Living in the wild and being close to nature and the people you love has a way of lulling one to sleep. So it was in the valley, with the coming and going of the seasons. I became so wrapped up with living the life I loved that I lost all track of time.

Time caught up with me, however. It was on a spring day. I was sitting on the porch and thinking about the beauty of some mallards that were swimming by. Having just returned from their winter homes, they seemed to have smiles as they swam, dove, and frolicked in the sun.

Mom and Dad were in the kitchen, and their conversation drifted out through the lodge door to where I was sitting.

"Have you talked to Rob at all about Whitehorse and school?"

"No, I haven't, Bill. I've been putting it off as long as possible."

"It's something that we have to face, dear. He's reached an age now when correspondence just isn't enough for him anymore. If he is going to learn a trade, I don't consider it wise to wait much longer. I'll speak to him and see what he says."

Dad and I did talk about the situation. Even though I realized that he was right, I found it hard to think of leaving our home, even for a short time.

"Rob, I don't want you to make any quick decisions. Give it some thought over the summer, and before fall comes, we'll talk about it again."

While it is true that all of us cannot be Einstein, it is also true that many of us do not wish to be. Yet there was something that my conscience was trying to say to me. I couldn't help but feel that yes, there was something that I wanted to be, something I'd like to do, but what? Dad had raised a very important question that I knew would not be easily answered, but answer it I must. During the course of that summer, I quite often caught myself dwelling on just that question.

On one such occasion, I went up into the attic of what was once the home of my grandparents. I had been seeking a place of solace, a place where I could be alone with my thoughts.

While stumbling around in the dark, I tripped over a small cardboard box and fell to my knees. To satisfy my curiosity, I took the box down into the light of the cabin and began to search through its contents.

The box contained a number of Granddad's personal things. He had written a few short poems; they were there. There was a copy of the New Testament, which was well read. The pages appeared to be almost worn through, and some of them were torn.

A tear came to my eye once again as I realized that I had never stopped missing the man. If only he could have lived long enough to help me grow up. I knew that we could have had a time together.

Once I'd regained control over my emotions, I began to realize that even though ours had been a short friendship, it had nevertheless been a close one. Without really thinking about it, I had never lost the memory of his stern, easygoing way. He was a strict disciplinarian yet certainly one of the kindest, most loving individuals I've ever had the pleasure to meet. He had the rare gift of being able to live according to what he believed, and he never asked me or any other to do something he was not willing to do himself. He could voice his firm displeasure, getting right to the point and giving a person a crystal clear image of his thoughts.

Without raising his voice, my grandfather could scold, discipline, and restore me and others in the family. He was slow to anger, and even when he did feel that punishment was necessary, he doled it out always with a spirit of love.

I continued to inspect the contents of the box I'd found. Coming across a copy of the King James Version of the Holy Bible, I opened the front cover. There on the first page, Grandpa had written, "To a special grandson on his tenth birthday." Well, Gramps had been gone a long time now, and so has my tenth birthday, but I will cherish the gift forever.

From that day forward, I began to read the book that Gramps had given me. Out of respect for him first and then because I became interested in the knowledge that lay between its covers, I continued to seek the truths that had been lost in the attic all these years. He had written a short note in the front of the book, which simply read, "Rob, pay close attention to the book of John, especially chapter 3 and know that we will meet again." During the course of that summer, I not only read John, but I also studied the entire New Testament and much of the Old Testament. I want to thank the wise man who was my grandfather, and I know that someday I will be able to do just that.

My parents had been surprised too by the discovery of the box in the attic. Dad was not aware of his father's devotion to the study of God's Word. Why he had chosen to keep that fact a mystery remains just that—a mystery.

Everybody has dreams; I am no exception. It took the friendship of an old man to help me realize what that dream was.

CHAPTER 40

JIM DAHL HAD been spending some time with us each summer since before I was born. This year he was coming to stay on the lake with us. He had given forty years of his life to the teaching of the Gospel. He was retired now and could think of no place he'd rather live out his years than with people he'd come to love. He'd considered our valley to be his home for a number of years, and he had his hobby, which was photography. Between the beauty here, his love of taking pictures, and an opportunity to bring God's word to the fishing parties, he felt he'd be more than content.

Jim arrived soon after the ice was off the lake in the spring of my sixteenth year. He came running down the ramp from the plane with a big grin, resembling a man in his forties. He talked a mile a minute as we waited patiently for his luggage. There seemed to be no end to the wait; however, the suitcases did eventually appear, and then there seemed to be no end to them.

We managed to transfer all his gear to the floatplane, and after a quick shopping spree, we left for the lake and home. We were no sooner in the air than he turned to Dad and said, "Bill, I hope you don't mind me buying Rob a camera outfit. I got him a good one to learn with along with a number of lenses that he'll need if he becomes seriously involved."

"If you're sure that you want to spend your money that way, Jim, it's your money."

"Rob has taken a keen interest in my hobby over the years, Bill. It'll give him something to do, and who knows, if he holds with it, I'll have a partner."

Jim and I had long been good friends even though only our summers had been spent together. Now, however, that relationship began to take on a new meaning. My interest in photography began to grow, and that led from one deepening commitment to another.

Through the summer that followed, the two of us were together good portions of the time. If Dad or Tom wanted a day off for some reason, then naturally I filled in for them. For the most part, however, I was free to follow Jim. I listened and learned many things about picture taking and about life. Through the months, as my commitment became stronger, so did my confidence. I found myself joining conversations and offering my opinions more freely. I even began to relate the newfound knowledge of my hobby to any and all who showed an interest. My knowledge of photography continued to grow with Jim's help and patience.

A number of years ago, Dad and I had photographed a caribou migration. Jim had taken what could be used from that film and spliced it to other material that he had accumulated on the subject. The result was an outdoor man's dream, a beautiful combination of animals and scenery that few people ever have the opportunity to witness.

We ran the film from time to time for our study benefit, and Jim would point out a number of things that could have been handled better. By his explaining how things could have been handled differently, I'd come away with a better understanding of how to manage light and darkness, shadows, and other difficulties that photography presents. He tried to teach me how to avoid pitfalls and also to use these things to my advantage, and I continued to learn.

On one occasion, I distinctly remember becoming discouraged with myself. I was having problems deciding on the proper setting for a given situation. I had taken several different shots with as many different camera settings, but none of them worked.

There was a pair of whistler swans that nested in a bay not far from the lodge. I tried again and again to film them, but the location was poor. The sun never fully illuminated the entire location at any time during the day. At best, the scene was partly in sunshine and partly in shadow, the result being a glare coming off the water where the two conditions met. Needless to say, this was not an ideal situation for a novice photographer.

I was almost to the point of giving up and leaving the location to the swans when Jim commented, "You'll have problems in the future that will make this one seem mild, Rob. The ticket is to hang in there and beat this thing. It's only a temporary setback unless you choose to make it more serious than it is. Remember, boy, success comes to those who make the proper effort. If we try, only to fail, then that is forgivable, but to succeed without trying is impossible." So I kept on trying.

From the black cloud of discouragement that had crept into my life came a ray of sunshine, which was Jim's advice. I followed that advice and kept trying, and my perseverance paid off. I realize now that what seemed so important then was really only a small thing in my life. People learn from the small things as well as the larger ones, however; even now I continue to follow the wisdom that I was shown that day.

Children need models much more than they need critics. Jim was a model for me during those years when I needed a friend, support, and direction. My father was far too busy to spend much time with me. It is sad that too often there is a needless struggle between a father and son. One often holds on to power while the other seeks independence; if we could only realize that both can be available through love and communication. Misunderstanding locks out friendship, but assurance of equality keeps out misunderstanding.

I never knew my father well when I was growing up. Our friendship came later when he allowed himself the weakness of slowing down. In my early years, however, Dad drove himself relentlessly on; why, I'll never know! I doubt very much if even he could explain the reasons why. I had difficulty understanding Dad then, but I have always respected the man who could remain content in all situations and whose word was his bond. He still maintained that it's better to be disliked for what one was than to be loved for what one was not. Argument against that kind of logic is difficult.

CHAPTER 41

M Y PARENTS HAVE always felt that people should be allowed to make their own decisions. As I approached my seventeenth birthday, we mutually agreed that if I was going to be qualified to make plans for myself, I should finish my education. Seeing the merit in this, I enrolled to begin that fall.

Formal schooling was not my long suit. I had a lot to learn about the city, civilization, organizing myself in relation to large numbers of people and the people themselves. I was the proverbial fish out of water, and no one cared enough to help. My whole life had hinged on less than a dozen persons; now I was forced to bear the brunt of criticism. Child from the wild, they called me; people can be very cruel! "These things have a way of working themselves out," I remembered hearing long before.

The months came and went, and things did get better as they always do. Soon I was tolerated, then I detected the odd smile, and soon the conversation began. Once we began to communicate, the icebergs melted, and one then two friendships began to grow.

Jim had said, "Never pay life the compliment of taking it too seriously." That may well be, but when you're seventeen in a strange place with no one to talk to, it's hard to appreciate the wisdom of that statement. I was glad the cold war was over.

My situation continued to improve, and I began to concentrate more on my studies and less on my problems. The days went quickly, the nights slowly, but June did come, and with it came summer vacation. Two months of freedom to fish, hunt, explore, and laze about the valley with really nothing to do except have fun. *Wrong!*

When I arrived home, it was a Saturday evening. We talked well into the night, and I was played out when finally we went to bed.

I woke with a start as Dad shook me. "Come on, lazybones. Rise and shine. There's a whole new day out there just waiting to be discovered."

Shaking off the cobwebs that clouded my mind, I swung a leg over the side of the bed. "I was under the impression that I am on holidays. What is this?" I said.

"There are no holidays on the river till winter. You had your holiday at school."

He was serious; I worked that whole summer. Six days a week, Monday through Saturday I fished, built cabins, and cut hiking trails. Sunday was the only day off, and even then, we didn't sleep in. We were up at seven, hauled water, chopped wood, fed the dogs, and had breakfast before eleven. We then gathered with any fishermen who cared to join us around the table in the lodge and listened to Jim Dahl read from the Word of God. Life settled into a routine, and the summer went quickly.

I returned to school in the fall still determined to be a photographer. Because I wanted to be my own agent and handle the marketing of my own work, I would also need to take business courses. My idea was to make my living on the lake but with the help of a darkroom and not a smokehouse. There was much potential in the valley for a person interested in wildlife and other beauties of nature. I saw the opportunity and pursued it.

As the months went by, I became more convinced that photography was my calling. The harder I worked, the faster the time went. Soon I graduated high school and entered college and began laying the foundation that would lead to my becoming a self-employed photographer.

The first year at college proved to be the longest year of my entire life. Vancouver was just the opposite of the life I'd always known and become accustomed to. The bumper-to-bumper traffic and the "I've got no time" attitude seemed to be an exercise in futility. People were always in a hurry and going nowhere; who can understand it?

Again, with time, I was able to blend in, and I too was living in the fast lane. I found myself longing for the slow pace at home many times, and doing so only added to my loneliness. I was so thankful for parents who cared, friends who'd helped along the way, a grandfather who taught me so very much, and Jim who brought it all together. I'd been truly blessed, and I was missing them all. It's strange how tears put a new perspective on things. We sorrow, we cry, and then we are ready to face the next hurt that will surely come.

By the time June arrived, I was well ready to go home. When I stepped down from the plane in Whitehorse, Mother was there to greet me, and Pop soon joined us. It had never occurred to me before, but my parents were aging. This was the first time I remembered Dad with gray hair; Mom too was graying around the temples. Life slips away from us slowly at first, so we hardly notice then how quickly the good years are gone.

If meeting my parents at Whitehorse had been a shock, I was in for a bigger one. We arrived at the lodge, and there standing on the dock was Jim. It was a full two years since I'd seen him, as his previous summer had been spent with his relations in Dawson Creek. He was seventy-one now and walked with a cane. He'd fallen on the ice during the winter, badly bruising his hip, and it had been slow to heal. He moved slowly and remarked that he could no longer sit for extended periods. He still loved to go fishing but had to go ashore periodically to stretch his legs. He'd kept himself occupied with his camera and fishing rod, but he was happy to see me come home and said so. I appreciated that!

Dad had scaled his business down this year. He no longer booked as many fishing parties, and the size of each party had been reduced. He also left two weeks free so we could have a holiday ourselves. We all needed more time for relaxation and were thankful for it. That summer I came to know my parents and Jim better than I ever had before. I could see that time was catching up with all of us and we had to make the most of what was left. I was not alone in feeling these things although I think Dad was most concerned about it. He said, "I'll sure be glad when you're finished with your schooling. One more year, I thought it would never end."

Summer rapidly came to a close, and as I boarded the plane to return to Vancouver, I heard geese calling. I remember commenting as I looked up at a perfect V winging its way southward in a clear sky. "Snow's going to come early this year," I said, and Dad shivered at the idea.

"Don't suppose there'll be much snow where you are, but maybe next year."

"Yes, I do hope that this is the last year. I am actually looking forward to spending winter on the lake once more. Just think turkey, mashed potatoes, cranberry sauce, and gravy. Do you have any idea how spoiled you are?" We all laughed, said our good-byes, and I left them standing there together.

Isn't it strange how much time we spend saying good-bye to those we love? Jim had insisted that he come along and see me off. I remember thinking then, he had said earlier that brotherhood was a condition of the heart and not only of the blood. At that moment, I fully agreed, for I had come to love him myself, and thanked God for sending him to us when I needed him most. As I laid my head back and closed my eyes, my mind held on to the picture of them smiling and waving their hands good-bye. These three people meant more than the world to me; they were my life. Little did I know that never again would I see them all together, laughing and carrying on, joking, and having a good time.

CHAPTER 42

WINTER DID COME early on the lake. The mercury plunged on the tenth of September and stayed buried. The snow piled up, and the wind blew; the dogs stayed curled up under the drifting snow for days at a time. They would appear only when hunger forced them to. Out they'd come from their cocoons into the terrible conditions just long enough to wolf down some frozen fish, then back they'd go again. Before long the wind would cover them with snow once more, and again they'd remain for days sheltered from the elements.

The wild animals, however, were not quite so fortunate. No one had stored up a quantity of food for them before winter's icy grip ruled the landscape. They were forced to forage for food in the deep snow, and before they could reach the ground, the wind covered up their efforts. Once again it was the large animals that suffered the most. Their bodies were too heavy to be supported by the drifts that were packed by the driving wind. Their legs were cut by the constant chaffing of breaking through the crusted snow. Their situation was desperate, and as always, the young fell first. The lighter predators had a field day; they'd run along the snow's surface and overtake any and all those they chose to prey on. Once again the moose population suffered great losses.

The winds stopped sometime in late October, but the hard pack remained. The condition that those weeks had produced plagued the moose population throughout the winter. They'd come close to the lodge, remaining for days almost as if they were asking for help. There was nothing that anyone could do, however, and eventually they'd go on their way.

It was near Christmas before the weather began to show improvement. The snow stopped falling for a few days, and the temperature became less severe. Dad was concerned about the dwindling supply of dog food so he decided to go ice fishing to restock it.

He harnessed up the team, hooked on to the ice shack, and pulled it out onto the lake. The hut had been built on sled runners and was used specifically for fishing through the ice. Up north a man needs protection from the elements. Standing on a lake without any shelter would subject his flesh to frostbite within minutes regardless of proper clothing. Our ice shack was six feet long and six feet wide with a chair in one end and a small airtight heater in the other. Between these two was a hole in the floor through which the ice auger could be used to drill the hole. We'd sit for hours comfortably providing meat for the dogs and for our table. Jim used to be especially fond of this chore; it gave him a chance to catch up on his reading.

On this occasion, however, Jim was not feeling up to the task, so Dad volunteered, not knowing how long it would be until weather conditions would again permit it. He grabbed the fishing tackle and a lantern and left the cabin.

Normally Dad took his rifle with him at all times, but this day he did not. Once the shack was set up, he walked up to the cabin for his fishing tackle, bait, and a thermos of coffee. He noticed the rifle hanging over the mantle but shrugged off the idea. When he left the cabin, something was bothering him, but he knew not what. As he approached the fishing shack, he looked up and saw a black object moving about. It was some two miles away, near the mouth of the river. He said to himself, "There's one animal that isn't dead yet," and went into the shack. The hours went by, and he thought no more of it.

Today the fish were hungry, and the box was almost full; it had been a good day. The wood box was getting close to being empty, and soon he would call it a day.

When the wood was gone and the temperature dropped in the shack, Dad picked up the fish box and started for the house. He'd come back tomorrow and fill the wood box for the next time. He walked outside into the darkness of a Yukon evening in December.

The stars were out in a clear sky, and the northern lights swept in bars of color. They shimmered and danced across the expanse and were highlighted by the stars. The top of the snow at sixty below glistened in the moonlight. Light shone through the window of the cabin and shimmered on the hoar frost that hung in the air. *How peaceful*, he thought, *how lovely this piece of land of ours in spite of the short days and long nights.* I suppose he might have stood there longer, enjoying the beauty that was a reality in spite of the cold, but it was not to be.

He received very little warning of the animal's presence, just enough to shield his face. The smell hit him first—wolverine. A chill ran down his spine as the full weight of the animal hit the top of his head. He had gone for Dad's throat but missed, on the way by the wolverine ripped and tore, bit into Dad's jaw and then was gone as fast as he came. When he left, he took a fish with him.

The animal left my father wounded, but not seriously. Dad lay shaking from the shock of the moment and the cold, bleeding and dismayed. He was not damaged so much physically as he was surprised and exhausted from the sheer unbelief of it all. Oh, he was hurt, there's no doubt about that, but he'd been there before and would get over it. First though, he had to compose himself and get to the cabin, stop the bleeding, and get warm.

He came up to the door just as Mom was coming to the door to call him for supper. Stumbling into the light, he collapsed on the floor. Soon the bleeding was stopped, and the warmth began creeping into his bones; he recovered enough to wash up and eat supper.

That evening, he experienced some pain in spite of the shock of the situation. The pain was nothing, however, compared to his feelings the following morning. The animal had done quite a number on him even though the two had really only roughly passed in the night. The scratches at the back of his neck were deep and long, and at the side where he'd been bitten, the wolverine's teeth had gone right to the bone. Thankfully Dad had dropped his head and hadn't been bitten in the neck area at all but on the jaw. He would be badly scarred.

The animal must have been crazed with hunger; if it meant his life, he was determined to have some of those fish, and he did.

The days passed slowly while Dad healed. He was confined to the cabin because the temperature had dropped again. Until his wounds healed, he was unable to handle the cold; the damaged flesh would have frozen instantly. Before long, however, he began to venture outside once more for short periods at first. Soon life returned to normal for him, as normal as the harsh winter weather would allow.

Nearing the end of February, the weather warmed up again, and it began to look like maybe there'd be some light at the end of the tunnel.

This was the first letup of any consequence that they'd had since the bad weather began in September. Jim had been affected most; his health began to fail, and for the first time since coming to the valley, he became discouraged. To break the monotony, they all flew to Whitehorse for the weekend. They all needed to get away from the confinement of cabin life. It was there that he collapsed on the floor in a heap. My parents rushed him to the hospital of course, but he died immediately. "Massive heart attack," the doctor said later. Jim had gotten his wish. He always said, "When I come to die, I pray that it will be quick," It was!

Jim Dahl was more than a friend to us; he was part of the family. He would certainly be missed.

Mom and Dad returned to the lake within a few days and began the task of putting their lives back together. Living without Jim's smiling face and jubilant attitude would take time and effort, but life must go on. It was not easy.

CHAPTER 43

SPRING FINALLY CAME, and in spite of it all, Mom smiled as the first flock of geese flew over the lake. "It's been a long time coming," she said as she hugged my father and breathed a sigh of relief.

A few weeks earlier, Mom had gotten such a thrill out of watching the little droplets of water as they fell from the eaves of the cabin. Never before had she been so glad that winter was finally losing its freezing grip on the landscape.

She walked outside and listened to the geese honking as they flew over. A tear crept into the corner of her eye as she said, "Just another month, and Robert will be home."

The sun shone day after day, and soon the snow was gone. The geese and ducks laid their eggs, and the sun continued to shine. Soon the young birds began swimming with their parents, still no rain. The whole valley was a tinderbox as the trees reached deep into the soil for moisture and found little. Young seedlings and other small plants with shallow root systems began to wither and die, and still the sun shone. Earlier the grasses had flourished with the moisture that the snow had left. It had shot up quickly to blow in the breeze. Dried-up ashen stems were all that remained now of that once-healthy growth. The forest floor was powdery dry, and only a spark would be needed to touch off a towering inferno.

Late one afternoon, dark clouds rolled in and promised to provide the moisture that was so badly needed. "Surely now our fears will be over," Mom said, and as evening approached, it looked more and more like rain. When bedtime came, the rain had not yet begun to fall. Mom and Dad retired, and as they lay there hoping to hear raindrops falling on the roof, they fell asleep. In the midst of the night, they awakened to the sound of thunder. Getting up, they both walked to the window and looked out as a bolt of lightning streaked across the sky. Understandably concerned, they walked out to the porch, no rain; their worst fears had been realized.

They retired to their bed once again and tried to get some rest, but morning came slowly after a night of tossing and turning. Dad awoke first and gazed across the bed through sleepy eyes. "I don't think we got any moisture at all, Donna," he said, throwing the covers off as he grabbed for his pants. He was halfway through the door before he had his shirt on. Standing outside, he realized that not a drop of rain had fallen, promises but nothing more.

Then he smelled it, pine smoke. His worst fears were now a reality. Before he even climbed the hill to look things over, he radioed Whitehorse. Upon being connected to the forestry office, he stated his location, gave the details to the ranger, and offered him the use of their lodge and cabins for as long as they needed them. When Dad hung up, he could hear an airplane motor warming up in the background.

He then climbed the hill behind the homesite. After all this time, it had finally happened, the one thing that could wipe us out. A forest fire!

The high point of ground in the area was about a quarter of a mile from the cabin site. Once Dad reached that point, he looked out over the whole valley. Off in the distance, he could see the smoke billowing up into the sky. Somewhere near Quiet Lake, to the south, the lightning had struck. Once a spark was struck in a dry forest, there was no stopping it.

Many thoughts raced through his mind as he sat there. This had been his home since early childhood. Sometimes it had been a tough life, sometimes gentle. Often unforgiving, never lenient when one came poorly prepared, yet it had been his whole world, and he continued to love it.

His mind continued to wander as he considered the hunting, fishing, and backpacking before the accident. It was then that he had such a love for geology, and so much of his time was spent looking for mineral deposits. He had a dream that maybe he'd discover the mother lode, but that was yesterday. Trapping had been one of his loves as well, but the snow slide had ended that too. Then there was the fishing clientele, which began as a means of making a living and blossomed into much more. He had been fortunate; he'd been able to turn his hobby into a successful and enjoyable business proposition. There were the animals too, the moose, caribou, bear, and the smaller ones. He loved the many memories the lake had produced, and he'd cherish them as long as he lived. A squirrel snapped a dry twig as he scurried along the ground. The noise brought him back to reality just in time to see it go running up a tree. Dad was standing before the squirrel realized he was there. Then the woods came alive with his chattering and that of his friends as they warned others of the danger.

Dad took one more look at the cloud of smoke before he went back to the cabin. Mom had lunch on the table when he came through the door. They were just washing the dishes when they heard the forestry plane buzz the cabin. They both walked down to the wharf to greet their visitors.

Returning to the cabin, they went inside and talked over coffee. Dad knew that the situation was serious, but he had no way of knowing just how serious it really was. The bush was so dry that it was literally exploding as the flames raced through the treetops. It was a crown fire, racing along the top, driven by a wind that it was creating itself. Since it began at approximately three o'clock, it had moved ten miles. At that rate, the men expected the fire to reach the lodge by the following morning, early. Therefore, there was no alternative but to leave and leave quickly.

The rangers departed soon after delivering the grim news, and Dad went to work. We had a number of small boats that were used for fishing. Into these he loaded all the small items that he could: dishes, pots and pans, blankets, anything and everything that would fit. He moved everything that could be moved as far from the trees as possible. Then the boats that were loaded with household effects were covered with tarps and taken out into the lake. They were anchored out in the middle on a sandbar. There they would stay until he returned. Or at least that was the plan. They had no idea what would take place if and when the fire reached far enough north to threaten the lodge.

The sun set in a bloodred sky as my parents loaded the dogs into the plane. They had packed their suitcases, not knowing when or if they would ever be able to return. Dad circled the homesite as they took one last look before heading west to Whitehorse and safety. This was not easy for either him or Mother.

The fire proceeded to move north, spurred on by the wind of its own making. As the tops of the trees were kindled, the burning embers fell to the forest floor. This created two fires really—one a flash flame at the crown, the other a hotter and much more damaging surface fire. Because of the dry soil, even the roots burned, and weeks later, the swamplands were still smoldering. Men battled until they dropped from sheer exhaustion.

The blaze raced on, hardly slowed by their efforts. Water and chemicals were dropped from the sky, men and fire tools, heavy machinery, and water pumps battled the ground fires. Because of the rugged terrain as well as the dry conditions, the drought had caused the firefighters continued to lose ground.

SID BELL

Soon the fire entered an area where there were no roads, and it was away. Without access, there was no controlling it. The only hope was to pray for rain, and they did. The rain came seventeen days after the fire started, a slow soaking downfall that lasted for three days. The crisis was over, but the damage remained.

It was August before we were allowed to return home. The dry weather had continued throughout all of July, but now as we made our way toward the lodge, the wet season had begun, and the rain pelted the plane's windshield as we taxied up to the dock. We could not have prepared ourselves for the shock we received then.

The site that had been our home for so many years was now reduced to rubble. A lifetime had been spent here; I represent the third generation to call the lodge home. Here where both Grandma and Grandpa had lived and loved one another and their family. Here where Dad had been nursed back to health after freezing his feet and almost losing his life. Chico and Laika were still buried beneath the charred remains of the meat cache that had burned and fell to the ground. Here Tom and Wendy had chosen to bury their oldest daughter. Just three years old at the time, she was taken by polio slowly but finally. Here too was the body of Jim Dahl, a man who was obsessed by the love of nature that spilled over to include all of God's creatures. He had taught me so much about life and love. A shale headstone marked the spot where each of them lay at rest. We looked through unbelieving eyes at the tragic scene before us. The tears began to flow as the truth slowly came home to us.

The lodge was gone, only ashes remained, many a hard day's labor gone up in smoke. The roof had been high enough that the crown fire ignited the shingles. Many a good summer night was spent in that building; now it was gone. As the lodge had burned, it created enough heat to set the other buildings aflame. Nearly everything was burned, gone. A pile of carbon and ashes remained as a testimony to what had once been a very successful fishing lodge visited by literally hundreds of satisfied clients.

CHAPTER 44

THERE WAS ONE ray of sunshine that shone through the cloud of gloom, however. When Tom and Alice were a part of the fishing service, they built their cabin away from the others, closer to the beach. All through the fire, it stood there unscathed. It stood now intact, sound as the day it was built. We were thankful for that. A small rowboat lay upside down on the beach right where it was left after Dad anchored others to a sandbar out in the lake. We put the boat in the water and retrieved the others. When the boats and their contents were stored in the cabin, we returned to town. There was so much to do before we could ever live on the lake again. The wind would soon begin to move in from the north, bringing the cold weather and snow. It was just too late in the year to think about spending this winter on the lake. Spring would come again to this valley, and I knew I'd come too, Lord willing. My parents had known many disappointments and heartaches here, and they were beginning to slow down. I was sure though that they would be back too; their memories were all here.

The flames hadn't reached the north end of the lake before the rains came. When passing that point, I can remember thinking, *It's funny how things can change so much yet really remain the same.* When my grandparents began living here, they carved their home out of the wilderness. They are gone now, so too was their home, yet the wilderness at that location remains unchanged.

As the evening sun sank in a clear sky, it shimmered on the water of Big Salmon Lake. We banked the plane and circled to take one last look at our home.

A Canada goose swam lazily with his family as they ate and prepared for their long flight south. A beaver swam with a purpose nearby, determined to put the last touches on his home before the coming snow began to fall.

At the far end of the lake where the Little Salmon River flowed out and continued toward the Bering Sea, a bull moose broke the silence. He jumped over a windfall and came to rest on the beach. He stood quietly for a moment in full mating display, sniffing the wind as a golden leaf fell from a tree and came to rest on the surface of the water. Satisfied that there was no danger nearby, he lowered his majestic head and drank long and deep from the clear, cold lake water.

A twig snapped, rocks scraped against rocks, the moose bolted and was gone. He never looked back until entering the trees. When he did, a full-grown grizzly bear stood on the bank. The water of the Big Salmon River trickled by him as it continued toward its rendezvous with the Yukon River at Carmacks. Once again I said to myself, "This is indeed home. I will be back."

The winter was mild that year, and spring came early. In June I returned to the lake. My parents would return also but only for the summer. When I reached the dock, I moored the plane and ran to the cabin, prepared my bed for the night. Then I dragged one of the boats from the cabin and went down to the lake. Getting in, I pushed it out into the water. Three pulls on the cord, and the outboard started. Making my way to the green unburned side of the lake, I killed the motor and just drifted. It was now late afternoon, a bit of a breeze was blowing, and I was glad to be back.

There is a soothing effect that comes over me when I lie in the bottom of a boat. As the stars came out in a clear sky, I listened to the waves slapping lightly against the sides. It's a gift to be a part of creation, a gift to be able to enjoy the wonder of it all. It's the silence and much more; it's the peace that comes from knowing that all things go together for the good of those who love God.

This night I was fortunate indeed; the moon gleamed off the surface of the water, I heard the haunting call of a loon, a beaver slapped his tail, and I knew that I'd come home. I knew that this time, regardless of the hardships that lie ahead, I was here to stay.